Summer of '02

A Novel
By
Michael Frederick

Michael Frederick

Dedicated to my brother John

Novels by author:
"WHITE SHOULDERS"
"LEDGES"
"THE PAPER MAN"
"MISSOURI MADNESS'
"SHY ANN"

Begin Again

It's June in 2002. I'm driving Traveller my motor home up I-29 toward Woodbury my hometown in Western Iowa. I thought summer would never get here. For six months I've been using my sister Karen's sidereal travel chart, sometimes going over a hundred miles out of my way in order to be at a library book signing in a town where and when I was supposed to get maximum book sales at my signings. Her chart worked much better than my logical mileage-saving approach. Using her chart, that was created by using my exact birth time and place and matching it with libraries where my books circulate has enabled my sales to double at the very least. I know this to be true because last November in Indiana I went off her chart for two weeks, going anywhere I chose, to save time, miles and gas, the result being very enervating and obviously not nearly as fun and interesting for me.

During that two-week period off Karen's chart, I got in touch with this 'force' that I knew well as a salesman in my youth. It was literally a push, a foisting tenaciousness that eventually found sales for me after hard work and dozens of prospects who just happened to buy from me, all because of this force I put on them. Force only works in a man's roaring 20s and 30s when his energy and good looks create good timing. Since I'm now 40-something: if it ain't easy—it's a force..and ain't workin'.

So, after this two weeks on my own, bangin' my head into Hoosier libraries, I was as tense as a cat in a Chinese restaurant. I called Karen on my cell phone and told her to plug me back into her chart. The first charted library she gave me was in Mount Carmel, Illinois, a couple hundred miles from me. She told me that the color on her chart that passed through Mt. Carmel was blue, which represents spirit. At that time I was really in need of a spirit level increase, though not at all interested in the Holy Spirit baloney she's always preaching. She laughed and said she's not my spiritual advisor; I know she was happy to be getting her $150 a week again that I agreed to pay her if the chart worked.

I remember driving Traveller with my sardine can Hyundai I named Lawn Boy in tow, up Indiana Highway 41, then taking route 64 into Illinois at Mt. Carmel. My spirit was rising just anticipating the interesting things and people that would come my way when on my sister's chart, not to mention the better book sales. My book 'Shy Ann' was doing well right off the bat. My readers enjoyed it, and were interested in following me, D. H. Dayne, on my journey (on the chart) to become this recognized writer, a writer/in.

To become this writer/in was not just this interesting backstory to me; I truly believe by following it—it will lead me to become a validated writer published in the loop. I believe one good reader will either discover my books, or, at the very least, if I stay on the chart, I will become a better writer. That's what I must believe, or I will fade with no energy left to sustain this arduous work of a self-published writer, a life I have chosen to live.

As I rolled into Mt. Carmel early A.M., I truly felt like I was ready to begin again. Had my mind done this? Or, was it Karen's sidereal chart? Because of this blue line that ran through this town on her chart I noticed everything blue: the sky; signage and other blue advertising; royal blue dumpsters that lined the street on garbage day; blue vehicles; and, anything blue in storefront windows. But that was my mind looking for blue, not at all what I was prepared to experience.

For some reason I parked at the Mt. Carmel library without even consciously knowing it was the library. Then I took this nap until noon, waking up rested and alert, far beyond normal. Perhaps my mind was awakening chemicals that believed more book sales and enhanced spirit were here in this Illinois town of some 8,300 people.

Living on the road was agreeing with me. And not just after waking from a great snooze and being in this zone of blue. Ever since I left Maine and saw the last of Ann from Asheville I'd been getting more and more suited to living in Traveller, my Winnebago Adventurer motor home, without even spending one night in an RV park. Since early October last year, I'd refilled Traveller's water tanks twice and dumped 'his' waste twice, finding those duties easy without hassles.

Of late, I laugh more often, like I used to, especially when I awakened in the mornings. This is a good sign for a loner who talks to his vehicles and his imagined readers. More laughter proves to me that I'm getting happier pulling Lawn Boy behind Traveller.

I unhitched my blue Lawn Boy and drove him around to give him a run, looking for a place to have a big breakfast in Mt. Carmel. Jerry's Café, six blocks from the library, was where I stopped Lawn Boy.

As I entered the little café I realized it has a blue awning over the front entrance. Then, I looked back at my blue car and felt that's why I drove it here instead of my affinity for walking. My spirit was rising, anticipating something good.

Jerry took my order at the counter stool. It was incredible to watch Jerry take my order, considering he was missing the lower half of his left arm that was scarred/sealed into a brown club like the unopened end of a tube of Braunsweiger. Shocking at first: to see him adroitly toss his little green order pad with his right hand onto his vinyl counter, then hold it in place with his stub at the top of the pad while he scribbled my order of scrambled eggs, rye toast with hash browns and coffee in some cursive code that only his cook/wife could decipher. After I told him my name is Dwayne Dayne I felt like asking him how he lost his arm, since I'm a writer and those things interest me. But Jerry surprised me after taking my order:

—Not bad for a lefty, huh?, he grinned, his dark eyes lighting with good nature.

—Yeah...how'd you lose yer arm?

I wished right then that I had Blacky, my black leather writing folder with me to capture this man's humanity that's only shown to strangers like me passing through town. In fact, most of Jerry's customers, he told me, in 23 years had never asked nor knew the story:

—It was my hand...and about twenty-five percent of my arm. I never lost it. I know right where it is, Jerry smiled. It's in a wheat field in South Dakota. I was twenty years old...reached under a thrasher to move a rock...and it got me...clean. Then Jerry demonstrated with his left stub:

—I jabbed it into my side to hold down the bleeding...and that was that. I had to learn to be right handed, he chuckled while attaching my breakfast order to a metal clip that his wife could read easily from the oblong porthole in the kitchen.

And then: this man Jerry was the lift in my spirit I so needed, knowing it right off when he continued:

—That thrasher chewed my hand so bad...I didn't want it back...so I left it in the field. When this doctor in Pierre was sewin' me up..he told me about this place in Minot, North Dakota where everybody in the town is left handed.

He said he was raised in this place...or near it...I don't remember.

—You remember the name of the town near Minot? I interrupted with keen interest.

—No, can't say I do. It's northwest of Minot...I know that.

—Why was everyone left handed?

He didn't know. I asked him and he changed the subject.

—I'm left handed, I said.

—I used to be, Jerry grinned, raising his stub off the counter.

All through Jerry's greasy but good breakfast I knew that just like that, after listening to a few sentences from a one-handed stranger, in this obscure Midwest town, my spirit was soaring into the blue. That's exactly what my spirit needed, this burning desire to live and discover something to write about that could hold my interest.

I could not bolt Traveller up to Minot. Timing is everything. A storm was coming down from Canada. I will consult with Karen and she will tell me when it's best to go. Besides, I have a hundred libraries charted by Karen, places where my books circulate far south of Minot. And besides that, the people who live in these places are looking forward to my visit.

I must thank Jerry. Thank you, Jerry, for giving me this chance to begin again. Thank you.

After working through April, Dwayne Dayne worked his book signing tour across Tennessee to Asheville, where he loaded Traveller with all his 3,500 copies of 'Shy Ann' held in storage. The extra weight hurt Traveller's miles per gallon significantly, but now he was fully armed with every last book. And he would sell every copy—no doubt.

When I entered Iowa from Missouri on 29-N, I knew Woodbury was less than three hours away. My winter and spring signings went well in Indiana, Michigan, Wisconsin, Illinois; and Iowa towns where they were most popular, though not necessarily the most profitable. And I hit about a dozen libraries in Southern Minnesota that were on Karen's chart. These were all towns on Karen's chart, places where I should sell books well (according to the stars). I found out from Karen that late summer was the best time for me to be in the Minot area, where one-handed Jerry said was close to this mysterious left handed town northwest of Minot, North Dakota. I did not know the name of this town, but Karen was quite certain that if I was there in the summertime, nearly all of Northwest North Dakota would be brown and purple on my chart. All Karen could say was, "Wow...purple is mystery and brown is love/home. Both are so powerful at that time for you, Dwayne. Around that place you are bound to find something interesting to write about." Then she said: "Einstein said there's nothing quite as beautiful as the mysterious." Since she was at work in the Tempe library I asked her if she read that Einstein quote off her computer now. She laughed. I was right.

There was nobody in my hometown I really wanted to see at this time in my life. Since my father and brother are gone...I now have little desire to see relatives or friends. I even told Karen I was not passing through Woodbury on my way to Minot. That way my sister would not alert anybody to my arrival. What they don't know...won't hurt 'em.

In many ways, for me, Woodbury was like Thomas Wolfe's Asheville. Like Asheville, my hometown has its share of grills, rednecks and knuckleheads. Of course, it has many good people there, too. But these same good people would eat my ungrateful heart out like a dog devours a piece of meat if I ever wrote really bad things about their town. Just as Tom in Asheville: I would be roasted alive, treated as if I had committed treason during war. It's a hometown code: When one of our own...leaves...then betrays—hate them to hell.

Yes, Traveller was cruising, with Lawn Boy in tow with ease up I-29N near the Missouri Valley exit just north of Council Bluffs, when I decided to ditch into one of my libraries to see how my books were circing. I felt good because I decided to ditch all my relatives, not letting a soul know I was back on this first day of summer.

I only needed that six-minute drive to the library to remind myself of all the people I allowed to rob my time, because in the past I had given up time selflessly. Not this time.

The only person I cared to see...was dead, my father. For six years he's been six feet under his headstone, across the road from I.B.P. in Dakota City, Nebraska, home of the world's largest meat packer. That will be my first stop, after the library in Missouri Valley.

All four of my titles were circulating well in Missouri Valley. Now: my head's into this cemetery visit. My dad and I were at the same Dayne Family plot just a couple of months before he was buried there. I could see his thoughts then. They were images moving in his throat under his tongue. Pride was the image I saw. Another word for pride is 'withholding,' the holding back of emotions. Pride. Look at the word. I see a stiff word that stands tall and compact, like some imposing structure designed to block free-flowing joy to all that use it, and to those in its way. I know now that I was telling my dad, in the cemetery, to keep his cool, because one day I would tell a story titled 'Ledges' and that he would live forever in it as a father who was leaving his young son for a long time, and it will be in another cemetery near Ledges State

Park in the summer when he will share a moment of wonder with his boy at the sight of a Christmas tree in that cemetery. And Dad, you will live forever in that moment in 'Ledges' as I continue to write this, the fifth novel I have published since your death. Though yet I have not had one agent, publisher, or producer who will read my books or screenplays, I will continue this quest to become a writer/in.

Yes, pride kills. But not today. Today is the day I have been waiting for so patiently. Karen said that Northwest North Dakota would be my best place for mystery mixed with home and love, but only if I waited 'til summer to go there. Well, summer's here, and I've been more than anxious for it to get here. All winter, despite better book sales from Karen's charted libraries on her computer, about half of those towns were a boring blur of blinding whiteness and bitter cold.

There were endless periods of stifled breathing in small town cafés where this 85° forced room temperature was blasted into my face as if coming from hell itself—making half the winter despised and energy draining, to say the least.

And there was the good side of winter in the Midwest. It became visible in Illinois in December and became obvious in Iowa in January. It was on and alongside the ten thousand snow-plowed roads that led me to these out-of-the-way places. They were not roads plowed like in the city, by a fleet of union men who were strangers trying to get done before the rush hour. They were roads carefully cleared by men from each county, counties bigger than most cities, and these were men who were born and raised in the same county. Family and friends would drive over these roads cleared by these men they knew and loved. Vendors would have to drive their trucks to these towns to deliver goods that would sustain their own during the year's shortest supply of daylight.

Now, as I drive north, I realize Traveller has become part of me, just as Lawn Boy, Blacky, and my old pal Henry, my old/worn handleless leather butterscotch-colored sales case, a trusty friend who rode Floyd's hip in my novel 'The Paper Man.' Henry held a dozen copies of 'Shy Ann' easily, and Blacky could be standing in

Henry's open side pocket as if he belonged there. This bonding with Traveller happened this winter during spells of wind and cold in Wisconsin. I'd returned to Traveller after posting a bunch of flyers in a dozen or so small businesses where I'd also sell perhaps a dozen books on the main drag to these businesses who allowed me to post my book signing flyer. This prowling, I called it, was usually about two hours of selling; half of that time was walking from business to business, getting my cardiovascular exercise along the way.

I would have these short/friendly chats with perhaps some three dozen locals who would tell every friend and relative about my signing. Talk about word-of-mouth advertising. Then, before the noon hour, I would find out which café had the best lunch in town, where I would get permission from the owner to leave my flyer at each table and/or booth before finding a booth at the back of the café where I could write up a storm.

As I wrote, I could feel them watching me, and hear their hushed comments after reading my flyer. For me, there was always this palpable way of knowing whether my signing was going to go over well. After five or ten minutes it would settle down to the usual chatter and buzzing about the weather, the afternoon work ahead, funny things said and done by people they knew, the upcoming weekend plans, and, always there was that pleasant genuine sound some local made when he or she laughed above all others; it was a sound that was telling his people that things aren't so bad, and, we'll all keep goin' along just fine if we stick together.

Onawa was a familiar exit for me. I took it a hundred times in my youth when I worked this farming community as a paper salesman. Now the exit is lined with billboards advertising casinos on tribal land on the Iowa side of the Missouri River, and, but a half-hour drive from my father's final resting place.

My father's laugh was the first thing I thought about when his image came to mind. It was a loud Irish, good natured sound that was so enjoyed by all who knew him. I told myself all winter that I would not dwell on my father's death when I was here. Enough already. People die.

This was going to be a fun and interesting time to begin again; the time to allow good things into my life again. I will laugh more, love more, and carry as little baggage as possible on my journey to become this writer/in, a published writer, something that would make me even more...self satisfied.

Frightful/Joy

Up here, in North Dakota, summer begins early, when all the snow is gone. That could be in late May, or, as this year, in late April. Here, steady winds blow 15-30 mph from the south when summer begins on the calendar.

It took Traveller three days to get here from Woodbury, because I wanted to get to Pierre first, the most obscure state capital I had ever seen before.

Pierre was one of the cleanest towns I've ever seen. No pollution, no heavy traffic on wide streets, and some of the most friendly people I've ever met at any of my book signings. Pierre was like those black and white photos I remembered seeing in my 1956 encyclopedia, with vintage cars and trucks here and there; there were clean square blocks of two-to-four-story brick buildings with easy parking day or night; and there was that innate conservative Midwest sense of order and aloofness.

The Pierre library would be my only signing until Minot. Karen told me that Pierre on her chart for me, has a gold line passing through it. On the chart, gold means health. So, for some inexplicable reason I felt better than usual once I rolled into Pierre. This made me want to not know what each color meant in each area until after my visit. That way I cold not blame my mind for manifesting what the chart predicted. Anyway, Karen's chart had certainly made my life more fun and interesting since I left Asheville in my brand new motor home.

The 'feeling better,' I believe, was coming from a sense of feeling good in my skin, rather, an acceptance of my aloneness. Like some happy geriatric, I had this satisfied smile or half grin fixed on my lips that curved upward as if I'd experienced something extraordinarily sweet to my senses. Some chemical mix was soaking into my brain, telling my head 'she' was close to me, and that we would find each other. There was no doubt about that.

At times when I was en route to a library, off Karen's chart, I would feel this sense of being off balance, or, like stepping down and missing a step on a stairway then angry at myself for not being alert and observant. This would come and go, and, since Ann from Asheville left my life there had been no significant episodes of spinning back in time. Maybe that was gone for good since I resolved that part of my past.

I took 83-North all the way to Minot, a little over 300 miles, just 50 miles south of Canada. Never before had I been so far north in the Dakotas. It felt like it was close to springtime in Nebraska up here in this town of forty thousand, about half the size of my hometown.

Minot people are robust agricultural conservatives of German ancestry, mostly, and as friendly as can be. And why wouldn't they be, when surrounded by clean air and water with plenty of nature with about nine people per square mile.

I parked Traveller on the Minot library parking lot even though Karen hadn't scheduled a signing for me here yet. I told her to wait until closer to the state fair in late July about a month from now. I wanted to rent a cabin but couldn't because I had to be mobile if I had to go to that left handed town that intrigued me. I had no clue how I was going to find this mystery town; I only knew that if I asked enough people...I'd find it.

So, I stepped outside Traveller with Henry riding my hip. Six copies of 'Shy Ann' were inside Henry, two rows stacked three high, a light load for Henry and me. Most businesses were closed at this hour in Minot, 6:30 in the evening, except a convenience store, gas station, drugstore, a couple bars, and my last stop: The Minot Café in the Minot Hotel.

In an hour I had sold five books; now I was hungry. Of the five sales and other prospects I pitched, none had heard of the left handed town that one-handed Jerry talked about last winter.

The only way to enter the café was via the hotel lobby, a dark place with rich antique hardwoods that kept the space darker than most closets. A squat/fat man shaped like an old Maytag washer, who smoked and wheezed and huffed bursts of air out his nose like an overheated bulldog was the owner/manager of the whole operation. I heard this man give his name when he answered his old switchboard at the registration desk phone:

—Minot Hotel...Eddie, he snorted.

The hotel's café was good size, with every square inch of it stainless steel and chrome, metals I knew to be conducive to creative energy. I sat at a window booth that offered a reflection of myself. Each booth had one of those glassed-in mini jukeboxes that displayed songs by pushing a button that flipped titles left or right.

There wasn't another customer in the café, and I didn't see a waitress or any employees. To my amazement the song sung by the Marvelettes 'When the Hunter Gets Captured by the Game' was on the music selection. That's the same song Jerilyn sang in my book 'Shy Ann' at Richmond's Ms. Virginia Pageant. And there it is behind the glass in front of me. Two songs for a quarter. I selected it twice.

Since I was alone I could enjoy the song without feeling self conscious. When the song began I started this kind of shoulder dance while seated in that booth. And I sang along with the Marvelettes, who made the song a hit in the 60s. I was truly lost in the music while dipping my shoulders with Henry next to me. Now, I know I was not alone. She had been watching me, though unaware of her eyes on me, else I may have shut down. Just when I'd spent an entire winter telling myself I was done with younger women: there she was, maybe 32 years young, with her intelligent/quick head turn that pretended not to be watching her only customer. She smiled at my embarrassment, but because of this immediate feeling that I call frightful/joy—I kept shoulder dancing while my eyes were on her black jeans and T-shirt that advertised the Minot Hotel. As she approached to take my order, I kept dancing and stopped singing not far from the end of the song. I read her nametag and smiled into her clear hazel eyes:

—Hi, Vee! I'm Dwayne.

She took my extended right hand in hers and pumped it twice and downward toward her. She noticed that my hand was softer than hers as she stood there with that perfect body that had a perfect

-12-

face...to me. I knew from a thousand missed opportunities I had to act now or be swept under that rug called regret as the Marvelettes started again:

—You like that song, she smiled.

She laughed when I began to shoulder dance, but I was self conscious now. This rare gem of timing, if she's single, even moves Alissa from Fredericksburg off the chart. Right away, I wanted to say, "Just think, Vee...if you liked me...you'd have two perfect asses...yours and me." Instead, I asked her:

—Are you from Minot?

She saw him look at her left hand; she missed nothing, but liked the fact he was obvious about it.

—No, she said above the music. I live here now, she smiled curtly, now ready to take his order with her left hand.

—You're a lefty! I had to exclaim. Me, too! We know what we're doin'...don't we? I winked before realizing I'd never winked at a girl in my life.

Her courtesy smile told me she wasn't rushed, just not into flirting now.

—Have you ever heard of a town near here where everyone in the town is left handed?

The look in her eyes changed to suspicion. It was strange. She didn't appear to be interested when I told her I'm a writer...at first. After she took my order she walked away. And there it was again. I had to say something fast or she would be gone forever, out of my life like some protean wonder that vanishes into the ether of conscious regret.

—Vee?

When she turned back to me, again I felt this stunning frightful/joy. I wanted to ask her if she feels this same terrible sense of loss coming if they don't act on finding out what they would be like together. Instead, I waved away my words and found myself thinking about the diffidence I called Shy Ann in my book.

She smiled while making his sandwich, and began to dance at the stainless steel counter, moving her shapely hips to the rhythm of the song that she also liked. When she reached for a head of fresh lettuce, as the song was closing, her eye caught him dancing with his shoulders. He appeared more lost in the song, especially when it was over and she saw him looking out into the darkness.

When she brought his food:
—You really do like that song, don't you?
—It's in one of my books. You know a good place to stay in Minot?
—I live here. It's clean...and quiet.
—You live in the hotel?
—Yeah.
—I was going to check into staying here while my motor home is getting serviced.
—The rates are good...before the fair. See Eddie.
—He's the guy I saw at the desk
—Yeah.
—I have to ask ya, Vee...what's a single person do in this town?
She smiled and said, "not much."

That was that. No hint of Vee the waitress being interested in a stranger maybe 15 years older than she. And this feeling I call frightful/joy, I'll have to write about instead of finding out where it leads. As usual.

Part of acting on it: I checked Eddie's rates; at twenty-nine bucks a night—I'd get away from Traveller and, I would have a shot at finding out if frightful/joy was just plain fear of rejection. But I did know one thing: she alone would make it good or bad timing; it all depends on where she is in her life. It's always up to her. I saw it in her quick/intelligent glance. Only the most beautiful and intelligent women can be that quick, so quick—they reveal nothing. And they are reserved only for men they are interested in. American women have brought it to an art form.

Since Vee's a younger woman...again...I can hear the cynical voices from my family, mostly from Karen lecturing me about meeting women closer to my age. I tell her that women my age are not out there, they're taken or used up.

After I'd checked Eddie's rates, finished my sandwich, and was sure Vee was not coming out to chat with me, I opened Blacky and began to write like D. H. Dayne:

The first thing that hit him, like a baseball bat to his skull: this waitress has the kind of face that men die for in battle; or, they run like hell—so they can see that face again. Now, having just met this young woman named Vee in Minot: he would be the coward in battle who would run, in order to live to see that face again. Easily he could imagine that he was in love with a woman like Vee in another life. A woman so beautiful it was hard to be away from her for long.

He could see himself as a lowly private from the Dakota Territory during the Civil War, perhaps at Shiloh. He was afraid he'd die in battle and never see her again. Yes, a man wanted to live because he dreamed of spending his life looking at that face.

I closed Blacky, paid for the bill she left when I was briefly writing, and left her a two-dollar tip. Then I hit the Minot air and pavement still thinking about her. Somehow this connection I have with this Vee today is related to whether I fought or ran, lived or died...in a distant past. This belief in past lives I realize may be my own lack of maturity, and that's part of why I'm attracted to younger women, women who have more raw energy to burn. And by God I have the energy of a 30-year-old, and I rarely see that same energy in women my age who are still available. If I can find a woman my age with my energy—I will want to be with her. But where is she?

Vee's kind of beauty is hard to be around in public places. Men stare, women stare, men want her. Women are jealous of her, so, they hate her—only because she is beautiful. So beautiful: there's always this half-measure in my attempt to describe her. The shape of her face is not perfect, for that's always relative what is beautiful to someone; but to me it's the pure raw look of a beautiful animal like a female panther in her cheekbones. And those almond shaped hazel eyes that turn to shades of green and gold in different light as if changed by some circumambient air that even made her long/full lips puffy yet diminished according to the pressure she puts there with her brow. A brow that's unfettered and smooth above the lush ash blonde eyebrows that grew so beautifully far across both sides of her eyes, yet not too close together to make her face sinister and cruel and stupid. Those wild and sexy eyebrows complimented her eyes and hair so naturally...it's erotic as hell to me.

Anyway, I'm infatuated again. If I end up with this woman, Karen's chart gets the credit; and, the long winter wait for Minot and that mysterious left handed town Jerry told me about—will be that much more fun and interesting for me.

After finding Traveller a service center with good night lighting I walked about two miles back to the Minot Hotel toting a gym bag with clothes, and Henry was loaded with books and Blacky. Along the walk I sold three books, including one to Eddie. Eddie told me that Vee's room was 312.

—Ya got a room on the third floor? I smiled while signing his book.

I was surprised when he gave me the key to room 311.

Before unlocking room 311 I turned back to the glossy dark wood of 312 and wondered if I should knock on her door and let her know that we're neighbors tonight. I knocked. No answer.

I liked my room. It was so like the kind of room I'd stayed in when I was a paper man in my roaring 20s. There were antique furnishings from the 30s and 40s, and a firm mattress. The carpet was dark and clean. The view of downtown Minot was the best part. I could raise the dust-free blinds and lift the window to get a taste of Minot air, and send my eyes out across the vista of lights of this prairie town once so dependent on the railroad. I forgot to ask Eddie about the Red River and if he had ever heard of a town of lefties. I heard that the Red River ran north and wanted to see it. If there was no such town...I may write about a fictitious one that lies beside the Red River. And I may name that town Jerryville.

After making myself a note in Blacky to ask Eddie about the

river and Jerryville, I heard a conversation coming from the other side of my door. Vee's voice was excited. From my peephole I could see her going into her room with a young man with short hair. I waited 'til her door was closed for a bit before I opened my door. Then, I stepped out into the dark empty hallway. It was laughter, the kind of laughter couples make before making love.

I went to Blacky to write about this frightful/joy again, and how this heart-fluttering feeling had to be related to some past emotions inside me, or some inexplicable connection to Vee.

Vee was her nickname for Victoria. Because she hated the name Vickie. She sat at her room's open window and blew smoke from a lit cigarette into the clean Minot air. Butch, her husband, was in the bathroom taking a much needed shower to wash the grease and oil from his muscular body. Butch hated his name, too: Gary. Butch was an Air Force mechanic stationed at Minot Air Base. Vee left Butch six weeks ago when she filed for a divorce; she left her wedding band on top of their bedroom color TV. Butch wanted to stay married. Vee has needs for Butch's body every two weeks since she left him. This is Butch's third visit to her room.

Vee's hazel eyes were looking out to the darkness. She wondered why she was so cold to that writer.

Minot was the only place she'd been in North Dakota since Butch was transferred here 11 months ago. She felt as if she'd been living here for years since she left L.A. Last winter she feared freezing to death if her car ever broke down between the café and the base housing where they lived.

Today, she had told herself a dozen times her divorce would be final in just thirty days. Butch said she couldn't have her extensive original collection of short stories and TV scripts she'd written over the last two years until their divorce was final. He reminded her that what's his is hers and vice versa as long as they were married. He kept her 23-pound nylon bag that held her stories and hid them somewhere on the base. It was mean of him to take her most cherished possession, knowing her writing was the only thing that really mattered to her; and, it was something that he knew would keep her here until it was returned to her.

No way was she going to go back to L.A. and trust him to ship it to her. Most of her stories were sealed and dated, registered by the USPS, her poor man's copyright in manila envelopes.

Oh, how she wanted to sit across from that writer and pick his brain about getting published, but no way; Butch would burn or shred her writing if he even thought she was talking about anything other than what's on the menu.

Inside her cigarette pack she removed a pin joint that Butch gave her, and lit it. She inhaled deeply, knowing it would help her cause to get her bag of writing if she had sex with...Gary, she laughed. She laughed again at the thought of calling him by the name his family called him: Gary Francis. Then she stopped her silly musings, for she knew she would never see her writing again if she mentioned Gary Francis, Francis being his middle name and surname of his mother's father.

Along with her husband's shower, her mind was running back to L.A. and the hustling she'd do to get her work sold to HBO, a network, or some cable production company. She learned her lesson. Marriage was not for Vee. And 'Vee' it is. It's official. When she filed for divorce she had her name legally changed to Vee.

Just then: she lost the image of her dream, and was here, in Minot. In many ways she now thought that Minot has the drab colors of a hick prairie town; but really she wrote about its true splendor and awesome beauty in four seasons of writing. So much more that is truly real is here, she knew. She wrote about what appeared like this gossamer green/gold of light for a thousand miles was this shimmering reflection of the land, this rich North Dakota land carved from glaciers sixty thousand years ago, land that could sustain ten dirty cities as big as L.A. for a thousand years, and yet, not one pinhead from the gluttonous city would give this place one thought of gratitude or appreciation.

She could hear no traffic rushing about; she could hear no sounds of faceless people trapped in city strivings—all wanting to be somebody, to be heard above the roar of the rushing manswarm. And Vee, she nearly cried out loud, you cannot leave without writing about this place, this place so far from the city, a place that gave me silence and the stillness to see that I was trapped in a marriage I created, all because I wanted to escape from the city, escape the madness...escape...to live.

Handsome Butch came out of the bathroom wearing his birthday suit. She was half-turned to him when she told him that this was the last time she'd ever be with him. Butch blinked that stupid look she used to think was cute, his mouth oval shaped showing confusion. Then, the thought of his mean act, taking her writing, brought her to her feet:

—No...on second thought...I want you out of here. By tomorrow at three when I get off work...I want all my writing in my hands...or your base commander gets a call from me about your pot consumption habits during duty...AND...the name of your dealer on base.

—You don't know jack shit, Butch growled.

—Airman Rico Hernandez.

She had him nailed. And the clincher:

—That Baggie...full of roach clips you kept in the garage? I hid it close to the gate by the big hangar where they park the B-52s.

—Vee, why would you do this? I thought we still might work things out.

—I want you out...now.

Vee went to the door, opened it and stood glaring at Butch with her arms folded in front of her chest.

I heard her door open. I'm waiting for it to close. Still waiting. I could see how beautiful she truly was from this pinhole drilled through my door. Even from behind this door I can feel this frightful/joy just by looking at her. It must be that visual appeal to my senses that triggers this frightful/joy inside me. Her hair: its texture and color are thick ash blonde with a touch of red in some strands. I know I would lose myself in wave after ash blonde wave that falls perfectly to the size and shape of that incredible face that I could see had my fingers trembling like a Canadian rat terrier in

January.

From the peephole I could see her waiting for someone to leave. Soon, I saw the same good looking young man exit her room with the same look of anger on his face. I vacillated whether or not to open my door to ask her if she was okay; or, to leave her scene alone, but write about it, quickly.

I started writing soon after she closed her door behind him. There was so much to remember, and I did not want to lose the weight of this frightful/joy that stirred in me just from the sight of her. Tomorrow at breakfast I will see her and hope like hell that the hunter gets captured by the game.

Heart of Mine

She finished her pin joint a half-hour after Butch left her room, and right after her attorney called her and told her that Butch would have to pay her four thousand dollars by July 27th, the same day her divorce is final. He told his client that a certified check from her husband would be on his desk by noon on the 27th, and that it's been confirmed by Butch's attorney. And he said her husband would have to pay all attorney fees.

—Four thousand dollars for eleven months, she whispered, again sitting on the window sill. Her writing in that nylon travel bag: she forgot to ask her attorney about it, but she was certain she had handled that with Butch. Her attorney also had her name removed from liability on their 2000 Ford pickup. The four grand was from the value of their house furnishings and the money she'd shelled out for half of Butch's truck payments over eight months. No children. Seven hundred fifty dollars in a joint savings account. Four grand...and I'm done being married to Gary Francis, she laughed. Certainly staying in Minot to wait for her divorce settlement for a whole month without a car was worth it, she told herself, adding out loud:

—He'd better bring me my bag of writing tomorrow...or I will turn his ass in (even though she made up that part about hiding the roach clips on the base).

Later that night, from my window, I saw Vee cross Bison Avenue wearing jeans with a dark blue belly T-shirt. She looked incredibly confident from this distance.

In two minutes I was breathing the clean Minot air with these powerful shots of frightful/joy tensing muscles and pulsing veins I didn't know I had. I had no idea what I would say to her since she was obviously in her head about the incident with her boyfriend in her room.

I didn't see her on Bison. When I reached the corner at Dakota Avenue: no Vee. I knew she couldn't have walked out of my view. After all, I've had more experience walking towns like Minot than most. That's why I felt naked, because usually Blacky and/or Henry were with me. Last time I was without one of them...I couldn't remember. Then it hit me that she must've gone into a store to get something.

When I turned to trace my steps on Bison, she came out of a drugstore unwrapping a pack of cigarettes. She lit one before I could take one step in her direction. She walked fast, like a L.A. woman. For two blocks I kept a half-block between us, mesmerized by that perfect body in motion. I still had no clue what to say to her.

From the way she smoked that cigarette with quick hits, keeping the filter so close to her mouth while she walked so fast I was having to increase my walking speed in order to keep the same distance between us. Closer and closer I got to her...until my mind raced back to that long Midwest winter behind me, and whether Vee is the mystery girl of home and love on Karen's chart. I must act now...or forever regret not doing so.

—Vee!

She turned her head and saw the writer she met at work earlier today. A good sign: she slowed then stopped on the sidewalk, keeping her cigarette burning near her thigh yet she angled it so the smoke did not hit her body. To me, she appeared ashamed of being seen smoking. Another good sign to me. I had no idea what to say to her from twenty feet away.

—What's up, girl?

—Nothing much. Just walking.

From five feet away:

—Mind if I walk with ya?

—I'm just going back to the hotel.

—Me, too.

We walked.

—Can I bum one of those smokes from ya?

Thank God they were lights. It tasted terrible and made me a bit dizzy as we walked and smoked in the 70° air. I said:

—I used to smoke. I only like to smoke once in a while. I quit buyin' 'em. They're too expensive.

She kept quiet. Not a good sign. Then I took action:

—Hey! I know! Let's have a couple beers somewhere. My treat.

She smiled and said okay. And that was good for me. Already I had accomplished more than I would've if I was off Karen's chart. I was walking, talking and smoking with probably the most attractive woman I'd ever laid eyes on.

She liked the way he stopped talking and observed the surroundings without imposing on her what he saw and thought. So many guys just talked and talked, afraid to be with that quiet space that gave her so many stories, stories she felt like telling this man about. After all, he is a writer.

—I write, she said when tossing her spent stick into the street.

—You're kidding...I mean...I believe ya...I just don't run into many writers...except at my book signings.

—You write all the time? she asked.

—There's a bar, he pointed.

We sat at the bar on stools. It was a typical dark neighborhood bar with a few regulars slouched over their beers on both sides of us. We liked the same beer. A good sign.

It was Vee who started looking into my eyes. She was telling me her divorce would be final in a month and that she had to stay in Minot until then. She mentioned her settlement and the writing Butch better return tomorrow. And she told me she's from L.A....Santa Monica. I told her I used to live in Culver City and that Santa Monica was a good place to people watch. She agreed with a little smile. I could sense that she didn't want to talk about her past.

—So...what's ahead for ya...when you're free again? I asked.

—I'm free now.

I was lucky I wasn't wearing my contacts , for they would've blinked right out of my eyeballs.

After our second beer we were having a smoke again on the same downtown Minot sidewalk. I told her that my room was right across from hers, and after breakfast tomorrow I was going to sell some books in Minot, set up a book signing at the library and the day after I was going to hit the road in Traveller and hunt for that left handed town.

—You think you'll find it? she laughed.

—Yeah! 'Cause even if I don't...I'll find it in my imagination.

She laughed. For her it was the first really good laugh she's had since her honeymoon when she faked a yeast infection in order to get out of having sex with Butch, who was drunk and obnoxious to her mother at their wedding reception.

—What's so funny? I asked.

—I'm left handed, too. And I've been into my imagination a lot lately. I think it would be a blast to make your living looking for a left handed town.

—You free enough to go with me?

This reminded me of Ann in Asheville. I flashed back to when Traveller was stolen by the tour guide with the ulterior motive to get her money. I could see Vee thinking about it: the fact she only cleared a hundred bucks a week after she paid Eddie for her room. She reminded herself that her meals were free. But she still didn't even know this guy. She smiled:

—I don't think that's a good idea. I don't even know you.

When we reached the hotel I told her I'd be in town a couple days. Then she asked me if I get high. I told her every once in a while. She told me she had a bunch of roach clips from her ex, and that it's the only thing she took of his when she left him. Then she said:

—Do you mind going inside after a few minutes? I don't want Eddie to think we're together. He knows my ex.

—No problem.

When she went upstairs I saw a parked car with a bumper

sticker that read: "40 Below Keeps the Riffraff Out."

When I passed by in the hotel lobby Eddie wasn't at the registration desk. I took the stairs instead of the slow elevator. The air in the stairway was stifling, it smelled like a rancid dishrag soaked in Pinesol.

I ducked into my room and brushed my teeth after putting on deodorant. I didn't want to look obvious and change clothes, so I locked my room and knocked gently on her door. She called out:

—It's open! Be out in a minute!

Vee was in the bathroom. I closed the door behind me and locked it. I wanted to ask her to come over to my room in case Butch dropped by. Clothes were hanging everywhere in the room. There was even a portable curtain rod like you'd have in the back seat of a car wedged catty-corner outside the closet door. The room was clean as if recent maid service.

Near the far corner I took a seat near the open window. It was right then when she came out of the bathroom wearing jean cut-off shorts with long frayed strands and a white sleeveless T -shirt that showed such big nipples for small breasts. She went over to the night stand by the bed, opened a drawer and removed a pair of tweezers and a Baggie stuffed with roach clips. She sat on the window sill looking for a roach in the bag.

—Wow..I've never seen so many roaches, I said.

Squeezing it between the tweezers, she lit it, her long full lips taking a hit before passing it to me. I dropped the tweezers onto the drab olive-colored carpet. She snatched up the burning roach quickly, then the tweezers, then she told me to sit beside her on the sill in case the roach dropped again it wouldn't land on the carpet. Then she added:

—Eddie'll charge me for any carpet burns.

—Look..I'm sorry..but I really don't want to smoke any more of that stuff. It makes me tired. I just wanted to hang out with you.

—It makes me tired, too, she said.

She got up and motioned for me to follow her into the bathroom. From the doorway I watched her empty the bag of roach clips into the toilet bowl and flush them down.

—There..I quit, she said.

She extended her left hand out to him as if to shake hands:

—When lefties shake hands...it's a sacred promise.

—Who told you that? I smiled.

—I did. Now..when our hands touch..I make my declaration

He put his left hand out into hers.

—I quit smokin' pot, she said.

Sleep came late for both Vee and Dwayne that night. Vee was in her room on her belly in bed, her head close to the bedside lamp. She was naked, under the covers, writing up a storm about the writer she met who roamed America in a motor home while using his sister's mysterious travel chart to become this so-called writer/in, a published writer.

She wrote about how she wasn't sure if she was attracted to him. Was it because my life is in limbo? she wrote. She wrote that she was considering going with this writer on the road to hunt for some left handed town in North Dakota; and she said she was not at all interested in reading his books or interested in him reading her writing.

Before going to bed she wrote: "I heard his song playing on the table jukebox. From the kitchen I could see him lost in the music like a boy, unselfconscious and present. He wore these glasses that complimented the shape of his head, a head that was not round or oval, but a little of both, like a man of European lineage with fine brown/blonde hair. When I saw his eyes they were enlarged considerably by the windows he peered from. I cannot tell for sure what it was that I saw through those two little windows, but I know that each eye was steady as if they had learned how to live well. Usually I've noticed in men a dominant eye that shines brighter alongside the weaker one. Not so with his eyes. They were a matched distance from the bridge of his nose, working together yet weakened by his prescribed crutches. Though he appeared as a positive, interesting person, his mouth was sullen as if he'd been disappointed too many times. Sometimes it's a stranger who can help you see yourself more clearly, more so than a friend can. This man, perhaps twenty years older than me, appears to have that uncanny ability to make me want to impress him with things I can do. I can't remember ever feeling that exact same way around my father. Maybe I did, but I cannot remember if I did. I am considering going with him, to get away from where I am and where I've been. I trust him."

I was close to going to sleep, but it was those lingering, tapering images of her fingers and nails when I shook her left hand; and when she held her bottle of beer in the bar. In that dark artificial light of filament and neon I saw the red polish that was faded like on the tiny/tough fingers on a doll, a doll that had been torn apart and weathered by violent storms. Her nails were short and jagged with chipped uneven closeness. And in her grip–it was all frightful/joy during her accelerated shake, twice, and away from me, toward her and down as if she had some deep communication there. I mumbled:
—She's terribly proud.

Mystery, home and love. Could she be all of those things on Karen's chart? I asked myself the next morning when I entered the hotel café with Henry armed with a dozen copies of my book 'Shy Ann'.
There were a dozen regulars and hotel guests splashed here and there. I paid no attention to them upon taking a seat at the same booth. I looked around for her. There was a middle-aged waitress coming toward me, a local who had worked here for twenty years. I can remember Vee telling me that she had to work today. I figured that Vee must be in back. Before the waitress came over to take my order I played the same song on the jukebox. Still no Vee.
The waitress told me that Vee was here earlier and said she'd be back later.

My black Rockports felt good to me on the Minot

pavement; I thought they went well with my favorite olive/cotton pants that I had made into shorts that reached my knees. A pea-green short-sleeved cotton shirt was a good color on me and went well with Henry's worn butterscotch. I wore my new light silver-rimmed glasses that gave me the look of a middle-aged writer.

Eddie had bought two more books at ten bucks each when I left the hotel after paying him for another night. Minot was a clear 75°. Perfect selling weather. Traveller was a mile or so down Bison, so I would work toward him and pay for the service work done. I knew they'd let me park on their lot for another night.

My first call was at a tire store across from Eddie's hotel. The manager was on his phone behind his counter when I came in. Eventually the man bought a copy of 'Shy Ann' for his wife and gave me a tip: that I should get a booth at the state fair in Minot.

Stops 2 and 3: I sold a copy to each, a feed store and a plumbing fixture business. Call 4: I walked away with no sale at a ceramic shop. Also, none of those calls had heard of Jerry's left handed town.

Usually I would look quick inside the business before I walked in, to make sure my prospects weren't too busy with customers or with another salesman.

Right when I pushed open the beauty shop's door–I saw her. Vee was sitting at one of the three stations getting her hair cut. She was the only customer in the joint. Vee saw me but kept still. A middle-aged woman talked as she stayed with Vee in her mirror. My face was a bit flush from this surprise and the fact that Vee pretended not to know me when I said:

—Hi!

—Whatcha got, honey? the owner asked, still cutting and combing Vee's beautiful hair.

—I'm a writer sellin' copies of my novel. Do you read novels?

—I used to. No time to read much lately. Too busy.

—I read, Vee smiled at me in the mirror.

I reached into Henry and handed Vee and her hair stylist a copy of my book. After they read the back cover Vee asked:

—How much is it?

—Ten bucks. I'd love to sign one to ya.

Vee peeled a ten from her pocket and said to her stylist:

—Mary, you should get one, too...if he'll sign it.

I asked Vee what her first name is and signed two books just like that as Mary got ten from her till. I left the shop as high as a kite thinking how she helped me sell to Mary.

The energy Vee gave me emptied Henry long before I reached Traveller. I wanted more of that kind of high. That same feeling that made my heart so alive with frightful/joy was now mixed with this fluid invincibility that every prospect would buy from me. It was soaked into my every joint and curving my lips to smile, making me a winner in this territory of the north.

When I spotted Traveller in the service center parking lot, a great idea came to me. I would put it out there and see what happens.

After signing for the service work on Traveller I sat on my leather recliner and called Karen on my cell phone at her work at the library in Tempe:

—Hey, Sister Karen! Can you talk now?

—Yeah.

—You were..or your chart was right again. Not long after I arrived in Minot I met this waitress..Vee. She's really a beauty.

Karen was listening from her desk chair, her back and neck were giving her a lot of pain; she was due to get another cortisone injection.

—Anyway, she's a writer! She's waiting for her divorce to be final.

—Is she from Minot?

—L.A.

—How old is she?

—I think she's over thirty. I don't know. Not too young.

—Too old for you, Karen teased.

—Very funny. She might go on the road with me until her divorce is final.

—You work fast, bro.

—Ya know...this time I did. Otherwise..nothin'
happens..and I'm alone all the time.
　　　　—Yeah, she agreed. Do me a favor, Dwayne. Find out
when and where she was born.
　　　　—Why?
　　　　—She has to match with your chart in Minot..or it's a bad
match.
　　　　—All I know is she's a knockout..and I give credit to you
and your chart for putting me up here to find her so fast. Did you
get your check for June?
　　　　—Yes..thanks.
　　　　—I want to look for that left handed town around here..if
it's here. I hope she goes with me. She's a lefty, too, Karen. Oh..I
don't want to do any signings for a while. I'll sell door to door..
write more..with her, I hope. Don't worry..I'm still payin' ya for
July..just for findin' Vee for me.
　　　　—Try to get her exact time of birth with the date and place.
　　　　—Exact time? Karen, I don't even know her.
　　　　—It helps for a good reading on the chart. Just try to get it,
okay?
　　　　—Yeah..okay. What's new with you? How you been
feelin'?
　　　　—Rough lately. My neck and shoulders are really bad.
　　　　—I always hate to ask how you are 'cause you're usually in
pain..and it bums me out.
　　　　—Sorry, she laughed.
It was Karen's laugh that told her brother she was managing her
pain well and that she still has a resolute sense of humor about her
health problems.
　　　　—Well, Karen,..I gotta go. I love you.
　　　　—Love you, Dwayne. E-mail or call me with her birth info.
　　　　—I will.
　　　　I walked back to the hotel after getting the service
manager's permission to park Traveller overnight. I sold ten more
books by working the other side of the street on my way back to
Eddie's hotel.

When I entered the café to have lunch, my song began playing. Vee had her back to me while she was wiping my table with a towel. She was dancing with her shoulders. Her hair looked just a tad shorter, lush and clean. I found out she was so happy because Butch had returned her bag of writing. It was waiting for her behind Eddie's desk when she returned from getting her hair done. I watched her move that perfect ass to the Marvelettes. God, she looked good to me; she appeared to be in such good spirits when I said:

—Give me your left hand.

She smiled when I put a ten-dollar bill in it and closed her fingers around it while saying:

—That's for the book you bought.

I sat down, and before she could say a word:

—If you try to give it back..I'll just leave it for a tip.

She smiled and put the money in her front apron pocket.

—Have you decided if you're going to join me on the road?

—I'm thinkin' about it.

—Here's somethin' to think about: I'll give ya a hundred bucks a week..if ya help me with my research..if you go with me tomorrow. Think about that.

I could see her eyes light up when I made that offer. It was beautiful.

—What kind of research?

The look in her eyes was so attractive, but I tried to suppress my embarrassment and awkward attempt at flirting; then, I let it go, until I felt my ears ready to burst from fresh blood. I let her see my blush. It was something I learned in Asheville, to own the feeling, to integrate it and empower me versus holding the energy back. Own the feeling. "It's mine! I roared within.

After an awkward ten seconds that seemed like an eternity to me, after the hot wave of emotion left my countenance, I was suddenly swept away from the compassion I saw in those hazel eyes. I hadn't see such a safe place in a very long time. It was there for me to say anything I felt. But she surprised me:

—I'd like to go with you..and do some writing. I need the

money..so..I'll take your offer. Can we leave tomorrow morning?

I knew I would sleep in those dreaded ten-minute stretches of half-sleep all night long. I always did that when anxious about tomorrow. Around 7 P.M. I knocked on Vee's door. She let me in. She was wearing a T-shirt that covered her panties.

—I'm gonna get some things at the store for the road. Wanna go with me? I'll show ya Traveller.

I could see her, behind her half-open closet door pulling on a pair of shorts, her thighs so strong and feminine. To me she appeared anxious, too, not because of going on the road with a new man, or a writer. It was as if this was a much wanted step on the way to a better place. And that was okay with me. Better than nothin'. She told me to wait outside the hotel for her.

When I passed Eddie in the lobby he was reading my book at the registration desk. I wanted to pass by my reader without saying a word. I did.

Outside the hotel, I waited for ten minutes; then, she came skipping out the front door as if she'd won the lottery. I couldn't help but notice she'd changed clothes, into a pair of beige, light sailing pants with frayed cuffs that came half way up her calves. On her left hip below her baby blue belly shirt was a faded red and blue tattoo. As we walked I asked her what that tattoo is.

—A wishing well. On my 15th birthday my dad said I could have anything I wanted. So I got this wishing well.

—Does your dad have tattoos?

—He had a bunch from when he was in the service. I wrote a short story about getting my wishing well.

—I'd like to read it.

—Maybe sometime. You really like selling your own books, don't ya?

—It's how I make money.

—But you really enjoy it.

—It's what I want to do now.

—Wouldn't it be easier to have a publisher?

—Look, I want to make one rule between us. That you

don't ask why I'm self-published and why I sell my books this way. Unless you ever want to publish your own work. Then I'll help ya all I can. Okay?

—Okay.

—I get tired of explaining myself. For me..it's like explaining everything about a story I'm workin' on. Pretty soon..there's nothing left to discover. It's my way of holding my interest in the whole process.

—I totally understand..D. H. Dayne, she laughed. I'm the same way with my writing. I have no desire to talk about them at all.

—Short stories are similar to writing screenplays. They're full of this compact energy.

—Yes, but I've never written a script. I've heard it's the hardest genre to write.

—Yeah, it is. Much more focused thinking is involved. Every word about action, exposition or dialog has to have importance and visual integrity for the viewer. I like novels because I can get lost and recover when I want to. There's more freedom.

—You can help me write, she said.

—Oh, no..you have to do that yourself. I can read your work and encourage you to keep writing. That's about the only way I can help you. But you have to do all the work. And I would know nothing about what's good or bad for you. Just write.

—So, we'll be like roommates for a month.

—Yeah.

She asked if we could walk faster because the pace was too slow for her.

We walked faster, saying nothing for about a block. When we talked I was more out of breath, so I let her do most of the talking. I decided not to tell her about Karen's chart yet, for I still wasn't sure if she had anything to do with why I'm here. Love, home and mystery, Vee could be none of those things for me as far as I knew now. And I wondered how I would even know as we walked fast and made plans how we could leave Minot after Eddie paid her up to date tomorrow morning, and I told her to bring as few clothes as possible.

I stepped up into Traveller first via the side door in order to turn on lights. I watched her reaction; I was really proud of my home.

—This is Traveller, I smiled like a proud father as I saw her eyes scan the clean gold/brown Formica floor.

—This is nice, she smiled.

—I like it.

She went from front to back touching everything, even sitting on the recliner, the sofa, and at the dining booth. Then she discovered my queen-sized bed in the bedroom after ducking in and out of the bathroom.

—You have a TV in the bedroom and up front.

This was a big thrill for me since I hadn't had a woman in my motor home since Ann in Asheville.

—This is a vacation on wheels, Dwayne! I was thinking you had one of those silver breadbox things..nothing like this. She went up front and sat on the passenger seat:

—I can write up here! There's so much room!

Under the light at the table booth I opened my atlas and traced our route tomorrow:

—We'll take 52 North, up to 8, hitting seven or eight little towns jut a few miles from Canada 'til we turn south on 85, and after selling a few books I should find out if there's a town of lefties. I asked at least twenty people today..and nobody had heard of it. It probably doesn't exist..or some of those people would've known about it.

—Then you can make up a town. That's better, I think.

—Why's that?

—'Cause nobody will sue ya if ya write about it.

—I never thought about that. Yeah..there's always some attorney to make something of nothing. I think it's a good story if it's fun and unusual..no matter what we find.

—Hey, I know! You can title it 'For Lefties Only'. Then all the right-handers will want to read it, she laughed.

I laughed, too, like I used to. That's a good sign.

—You might have something there. I could put a warning on the cover: 'Don't Read This–Banned by the Pope'.

And she laughed like she used to. A better sign for him.

It was there at Traveller's booth we made a plan. We would make this month a left handed month. For a hundred bucks a week she would write down our insights and comments about anything related to:

—Leftness! she laughed.

We laughed and shook left hands across Traveller's table, agreeing to have fun as:

Karen couldn't sleep. She had a bad dream. It was about her brother Dwayne and this new girl in his life. In her dream: Dwayne was Ben, the main character in her brother's popular novel 'Ledges'; and this Vee, she was Darlene, the wild girl in 'Ledges' who manipulated Ben and nearly got him killed for the things she made him do.

This couldn't wait. Karen got out of bed and paced about her bed thinking about Ann in Asheville, the abandoned girl in his book 'Shy Ann' who stole her brother's motor home and got the money from Dwayne that she wanted.

Karen decided she was paranoid about Vee and it would be all okay when Dwayne got her the info on Vee. Karen went back to bed and sleep came.

Now: Traveller is parked in the far corner of a Minot grocery store, four blocks from the hotel. We were having a beer while putting away the $200 worth of groceries I bought and listening to a golden oldies station on Traveller's stereo. I had opened all of the kitchen cupboards so Vee knew where all things are stored.

My heart overflowed with frightful/joy, that same positive energy I had while selling books in Minot. All winter long I had none of this kind of fuel. From November until Vee I lived on the dead fuel of making money to pay the bills, a never-ending cycle of sell, sell, sell; then: pay, pay, pay.

But now: Vee is here, in my home, putting away the supplies we would share. I watched her lean body reach and extend and bend again and again while letting her discover where things go. No negatives like, "No, that goes there"; and she did not want to ask me where things go. Yes, here she is, putting away groceries in a new motor home, going with me on a journey of mystery and possible romance, when just a day ago she was counting the minutes, hoping her life would change for the better.

She thought that a hundred bucks a week would not be too tough to earn, perhaps ten hours a week of research and writing at the most.

When the groceries were put away we sat at Traveller's booth across from each other with our beers between us. She wanted to tell Dwayne now how she met Butch when she was living her dream, studying to be an actor in North Hollywood. Butch was home on leave when they met in a bar in North Hollywood after one of her evening classes. She knew that she had let Butch sidetrack her from her goal to be on the big screen. And that's when she came up with her name Vee. No last name. She would not need a last name. Everyone would know it by now, if she had not gone to bed with Butch that night and been lured away by his dream to be a pilot and fly her around the world when she was a famous actress. Instead: she got Butch, the Air Force mechanic, transferred to Minot Air Base just before two feet of snow buried half the Dakotas and her dream.

And now, she was with this writer, discussing being left handed and what it was like for her, any ruminations, anything at all while craving a cigarette so:

—Scissors, irons and ironing boards, pencil sharpeners..are just some of the things I know are made for left-handed people. I remember in grade school at lunchtime sitting next to kids who were right handed. Once I tried eating with my right hand..spilling peas and carrots on my lap. It was awful, she laughed.

—Was that in L.A.?

—Yeah, in Santa Monica. I never thought about it before.. but it must be harder for boys to be left handed..because of sports and tools.

—I think that's why I'm so stubborn and do what I do.

—Because you're left handed?

—Yeah. Maybe you wouldn't even be going with me if you were right handed. Or maybe you would've never married..or married someone else.

—If that's true..then being left or right handed determines who you are..and what your children will be.

—Yes, I agreed.

—Wouldn't it be interesting for two lefties to switch, start doing everything right handed? I wonder what would happen.

—The story I hoped to find was in this real town somewhere off the beaten path..and everyone was left handed because they were forced to be that way by the elders. Because there's something about being left handed..in the whole town..that makes their town a better place to live..somehow.

—They could live longer! she exclaimed. Or be more loving..or crime free.

—I thought about that, too. But I thought something terrible in the town's past had to have happened that made the whole town make it a law that every resident be a lefty.

We brainstormed silently for a half minute until Vee blurted out:

—What if it was some kind of brain chemistry that the town founders started because they knew it would make their town this special place?

—An experiment? I asked.

—Maybe. What if it was part of some hundred-year plan to get worldwide attention or a bunch of money? No! What if it was this big secret..they were careful to keep to themselves..even pretending to be right handed to strangers..to keep their town.. away from...

—...the people who always wanted to be right!

—Yes! she laughed.

I left Traveller parked on the grocery store lot. We walked to the hotel talking excitedly about our musings and laughing about this mysterious left-handed town. We agreed to meet downstairs for breakfast at 7 when the café opened. Then I would get Traveller and we would load her things. She told me that Eddie has a luggage/clothing carrier that would make the loading easier.

Again, at the hotel, she went inside first while I waited outside. She explained that her estranged husband would not like it if he saw her with a man, but that he was not violent; and that she didn't want Butch to think she was having an affair with a man before their divorce was final, effecting waves regarding her settlement at the end of the month.

Our brainstorming gave me the urge to write, but not here; I wanted to write alone in Traveller, resisting the certain pull to her room. Besides that: my room smelled from a cherry scented carpet sanitizer mixed with the odor of moth balls stored on the top closet shelf.

As I walked faster and faster with a hundred images flashing in my mind of things I wanted to put down on paper–I saw Butch drive by me in his truck. I was positive it was the same man I saw through my peephole. Butch was a handsome young man with curly-short, dark brown hair and a stocky muscular build. I could see the Air Force mechanic smoking a cigarette with his radio on loud, playing a U-2 song. I watched him park his truck outside the hotel's front entrance. At first I wanted to go back to see if her husband was going to make trouble. Then: a protean mollification, or, changing softness came over me. After all, he is her husband, and it's none of my business; so, I continued on my focused pace toward Traveller.

Not since my book signing in Maine last fall had I experienced one of those past-life spinning episodes that had brought me to the pavement. I remembered when I was in Portland, Maine that if I could focus on my writing I would not spin out of control. But Blacky was in my hotel room, and my writing paper was yet a few blocks away in Traveller.

How could seeing Butch trigger a spinback, I asked myself

as I walked faster and faster, calling out every detail I noticed along the dark sidewalk on Minot's business district:

—No moon. Stars are bright and numerous. Traffic is light. A blinking red traffic light. Storefronts are clean and thrifty. Air is clean. No wind. Just then: I stopped to look at flowers through a closed florist's glass. Beside a framed portrait of the owner's family was the North Dakota State Seal: a lone tree in an open field; bundles of wheat; a plow; an anvil and a sledge; a bow crossed with three arrows; and a Native American on horseback chasing a buffalo. And surrounding the State Seal was the State Flower, the wild prairie rose. The more I looked into the five pink petals, the more brilliant the center of the rose became, its cluster of yellow stamens appearing to open, allowing me to see something that had to be related to Karen's chart. I looked deeper into the yellow center and I began to see what I had suppressed:

Summertime 1970: A night carnival was on in Dakota City, Nebraska. This was in the same small town where my father was raised and is buried today. I was seventeen; my first love, Bonnie was fifteen. I had known her since she was twelve, a younger sister of a friend. We were holding hands for the first time while walking through this carnival of rides and games and food vendors. For a carnival the colors were a dirty/drab and faded as if worn from a thousand summer days of Midwest weather.

It was a poor man's carnival: quiet with slow rides run by a crew of faceless drifters, mostly young men living on hot dogs, fountain Coke, ditch weed and low wages. I could tell consciously that I was not there again, yet I could really feel the same rush of embarrassment I was feeling from a teenage arousal as I walked with Bonnie and could feel the touch of her tender hand that gripped as if she'd love me. And I could see again her big beautiful teeth smiling at me, flashing happiness to be with me. She had no idea I was aroused, even as her hips brushed gently against my thigh. I was into my head about being seen this way by all those around us. I knew she saw my blush but she did not know why I blushed. She thought it was adorable and attractive and wanted me to kiss her often.

I waited to kiss her until at the highest point on the Ferris wheel. I was thanking God it was dark, for I had never done more than kiss her and was not free to mention my teenage problem. And kissing made the problem worse.

Yes, those were my terrible teens, as I walked faster and faster toward Traveller with the same problem I had on the Ferris wheel. Every step was a painful reminder of my youth. And then the pain went away, soon after I realized I had brought my first love to that town subconsciously to be near my father and his paternal heritage.

In Traveller, at the booth, I wrote up a storm about my recent experience in the florist's window. Then I wanted to call Karen and update her, but it was too late.

My walk back to the hotel was a blur of nothing in my path, because nothing in the present was as important as what I had experienced in that wild prairie rose. The only thing I noticed was that Butch's truck was still parked in front of the hotel.

Soon after I stepped foot on the hotel's third-floor hallway my fear about trouble from Butch vanished into egoistic disappointment and this deep sense of loss. Definite sounds of deep passionate sex were coming from behind Vee's door: the heavy breathing; the banging headboard and squeaking box spring; and even the distinct aroused penetration sounds made by lovers was there—under the sound of my heart beating in my ears, above those dark thoughts of betrayal and chicanery.

Before I could unlock my door I knew this was part of Karen's chart, again taking me home, to my heart, where such things are stored until released forever. I knew I had to experience this pain, wherever it took me, as I punched Blacky off the desk onto the floor when now all sound was gone.

Again, I was spinning, worse than at Appomattox in 'Shy Ann'; or before that when I held onto that tree in Blackstone just before Appomattox. Into the bathroom I ran, closing the door behind me, where I soon found myself staring at my reflection in the toilet bowl, dry heaving while spinning back, back, back, until I was there again, at the place where my biggest betrayal happened. I closed my eyes, wanting to see it, wanting to let it go.

　　—SHOW ME! I cried. LET ME SEE!

　　It was 1972. I was twenty, a buck-toothed sailor stationed on a docked patrol gunboat at a San Diego naval base. I was on my back on the top bunk in the cramped enlisted men's living quarters at night. Again, I read the Dear John letter from my beloved Bonnie under the overhead reading light: Dear Dwayne, This is a hard thing for me to tell you. I'm dating other guys, so I think we should break up. I know you were just here on leave, but I can't stay at home all the time waiting for you. I get so lonely, Dwayne. It's hard being so far away. Now you are free to date, too. This is the hardest thing I've ever done. I'm sure your family will hate me. Take care and God bless. Love, Bonnie.

　　I folded the letter, returned it to the envelope that was missing her perfume, and slid it inside my pillow case under my head after turning off the reading light. Then I inserted the ear plug to my cassette player and tortured myself with Chris Rea's song 'Fool If You Think It's Over'. Chris made me cry. That's why I played it over and over, until my eyeballs were drained. It was the first time I'd been able to cry since receiving her letter three days ago.

　　Last night I had the midnight to 4 lookout watch when we were out at sea patrolling the coast in choppy waters. I never consciously thought about letting go of the ladder on my way up to my lookout station, but my arms and legs were so weak from the shock of Bonnie's words and the ensuing fatigue, I could easily miss a rung, slip, and end up shark bait in the blackness of the deep Pacific.

　　It was my first heartache as a man, sometimes the hardest of all to take in and accept.

　　The next morning after my Chris Rea sob session, I was on

duty again at sunrise colors poised with Old Glory at the aft stantion that held the flag. The whistle blew, signaling all of the ships docked to unfurl the flag. Mistakenly, I had hooked the two ends of the flag together and tossed my country's flag into the water. Every ship has an asshole. The biggest of all was Chief Boorman, a grouchy middle-aged pinhead lifer who had the personality of a snake during a thunderstorm. He saw it as I stood staring at the flag some ten feet below in the dark green water. I began removing my shoes after slamming my white monkey hat onto the deck, muttering expletives until Chief Boorman stopped me from diving after the flag.

—Dayne, go get a boatswain's hook and fish it out, for Christ's sake! he laughed.

When I came out of my spin, face down in the Minot Hotel's toilet, I was laughing. The flag disaster had taught me to lighten up, that all things pass and to move on to other things quickly, because more shit happens when you hold onto old stuff. Then, a memory came to me with such clarity: Just a short time before Bonnie's Dear John letter, she had given me a great goodbye f..k, knowing on some level it was their last time together. And that's what Vee is giving Butch. Yes, she's giving Butch this last goodbye to say I loved you, and this is what you'll be missing for the rest of your life.

I began laughing. My silly ego came out to show me a lesson I'd already learned, and to drop that possessiveness mentality that never made anyone's life good, especially a man who lives alone.

I went to the open window to mitigate it all, to quiet my monkey mind that was telling me to leave now and not get involved in her life now. Perhaps they may reconcile, I thought. Some people like to fight and then make up, then begin again.

—Go with the flow, I whispered.

Then my eyes took in the peaceful summer night in Minot, raking my eyes across a thousand vanilla-colored lights, in a part of North Dakota that averaged two people per square mile. Soon,

with or without her, I would be scouring a land to which I had
never been. It will be more fun if she comes along, but I was
prepared to go alone. Being on Karen's chart was certainly better
than the life I lived before: shotgun book signings; the same
restaurants and coffee houses that soon labeled me a writer and left
me alone; and then, when I had read enough faces that told me I
was a loner to be ignored–I would move again, to another city and
begin again, submerged once again in this gypsy rush to be a
stranger once more, until the cycle repeated itself..again and again,
at least a hundred moves in thirty years.

    I opened Blacky and wrote for twenty minutes before going
to bed.

    I slept hard and deep for six hours. It was Vee's
knuckle/rapid knocking on my door that woke me at 7 A.M. Her
energy was like that of the dust devils I knew so well in Arizona,
spinning me wide awake while pacing around me with these short
bursts of wonderful words packed with such intense beauty:

    —My stuff's all loaded on two carts. I got my check from
Eddie already. Can we get breakfast on the road? I wanna get out
of Minot so bad, Dwayne.

    —I'll grab a quick shower.

    She watched him stumble into the bathroom in his boxers.
She thought his body looked good for a man fifteen years older than
she. The sound of his running shower made her even more restive,
until she noticed Blacky on the night stand by the bed. She went
over to the black writing folder and opened it after pausing to be
sure his shower was still running. The top page, in pencil, she
pulled out of the folder and read quickly:

    It was titled 'Heart of Mine' and read: "For the second time
in my life, on this porch swing side of my life, I thought she was
the girl who has been waiting just for me. She was true, only in my
mind. I could hear that perfect body making love to a man more
handsome than I. It happened just moments ago, and it hurt me.

    I do not know her, yet I've been waiting in a thousand
places for her, pausing to think of only her at least ten thousand

times. And where could she be waiting for me? I realized last night: it's a trap. More so an American trap. To live happily ever after. Bullshit.

Now, all I know, whether she will love me one day or not, no matter how sweet and loud the music between us–I will hear her with another man, a man much better looking than I. I must sleep now, knowing well that no sleep will release it from this brain now poisoned with the memory of sounds that are also mine. Oh, damn this heart of mine.

The Corner Café in Coulee, North Dakota was the first breakfast place I saw, 36 miles northwest of Minot on 52 and 50. Traveller was longer than the café and literally blocked the morning sun from shining in the café's front window. D. H. Dayne signed two books at $10 each; it paid for their meal and a good tip. Our waitress had never heard of a left-handed town; she went back and asked the owner. Same answer.

They had been quiet over breakfast. His words she read in Blacky made her shut down. She hadn't told him she read his work. Who would? she had told herself.

Outside the café:

—Let's walk a bit, huh? I said.

I led the way, off the main drag, onto the paved residential street with no sidewalk. We walked down the middle of the quiet street that was sparsely lined with old weather-beaten single-floor homes that were painted a dull white mostly.

She sensed that it had to be said:

—I really messed up last night.

She waited for him to say something. Nothing came.

—My ex came over. I slept with him.

—But he's not your ex yet, so you slept with your husband.

She could not see his eyes, they were averted; he was not coming close to saying what she secretly read while he was in the shower. She felt manipulative yet weak from knowing his true words. She continued, not knowing where she was headed:

—I know it's a self worth thing. I'm still trapped in Vicky

Derryberry's mind.

I stopped my laugh before it came out:

—Vicky Derryberry?

—That was my name. I hated it. All of it. Kids called me Dicky Verryberry.

—Yeah..they made fun of my name, too. Kids are cruel. They're parrots..trained by their stupid parents.

—So, I'll keep Butch's name..Cameron.

—Vicky Cameron, I said.

—Vee Cameron. I hate Vicky.

—Well, Vee..you still gonna divorce Butch?

—Oh yeah. That was just sex. It's the only thing he's good at, she laughed.

I chuckled and said:

—Sounds like you're both good at it.

She didn't laugh.

—When I heard you and Butch last night..I wrote about how it was a negative thing for me. But just before that I was looking through this florist's window..and I could clearly see this memory of me with my first girlfriend. We were at a carnival..in the town of my father's family. And I really felt this pain in my groin..like I was there again. See..my sister is a librarian..and she created this metaphysical travel chart using astrology, my birth date and time, and place of birth. She has like eight categories matched to colors. Blue is spirit. Green..prosperity. Gold means health. I can show you a sample chart she sent me. Anyway..she says these colors run true for me..and if I go to these places I can experience whatever I need in my life..with all these interesting people and things to write about..and I will become a better writer..a writer/in I call it.

—God, that's so interesting, Dwayne.

—I came to Minot to experience purple and brown on her chart. Mystery is purple, and brown is home and love. I believe the mystery is writing about this left-handed town..if there is one. When I played that song in Eddie's café it was the same song I used in one of my scripts and also it was in my recent book 'Shy Ann'.

Anyway, I thought you were the love for me on my chart, that I was home, where I supposed to be. Isn't that crazy?

    —I really think it's incredible. I want to see that chart. Could your sister create one for me?

    —I was afraid to give her your name. She asked me to get your birth info..because she wants me to be safe, I guess.

    —I'd love for her to find out all about my..stuff. Why were you afraid to give her my name?

    —For starters..I didn't know your name. And..I was afraid she would find out that you were not the one.

    —The love of your life?

    —Yeah.

    —Maybe I'm the mystery, she laughed.

    We came upon an open field filled with giant yellow sunflowers with their green stalks nearly three feet tall, and each core of every flower was a rich brown. The sunflowers were framed on three sides by fields of green/gold barley for as far as we could see.

    Vee led the way, picking up her pace until she was making these feminine prancing jumps, like a gazelle so elated to be alive. I followed her into this sea of undulating yellow and green until she reached the middle of the field. I watched her turning so slowly and gracefully in these small circles with her eyes closed and her slender arms extended out from her sides as if she were in flight just above the field. I was ten feet away from her when I could see her hazel eyes lighten to this incredible color of gray/gold until they changed again to a dark green. My eyes bathed in all of this truly lovely woman, from her small breasts to her exposed belly that was just above the most perfect butt I'd ever laid eyes on.

    Then, as she danced in the yellow/green it hit me like a sledge hammer between my eyes: I had found Josie my 'young girl' in my novel 'The Paper Man'. And she..just as Josie did..had come to me..to my room in Eddie's hotel, just as Josie had come to the old Pine Ridge church to comfort Harvey when he was the lonely son of a paper man. And years later, she returned to Harvey after they were lovers and she had been unfaithful. But could Harvey ever trust her again? That's what Harvey's alter ego Floyd was asking me over and over in the sea of yellow and green amidst this aching desire to let the image go. It was the image made of sound, the sound of her making love to her husband, that man that was younger and better looking.

And then: the spinning was coming back as she twirled her body in circles faster and faster..counterclockwise. This time: I let it go. I wanted to see where it would take me, all because I wanted to trust her and kill this lack of trust that would destroy any chance for real love.

It was like at Appomattox in 'Shy Ann'; before I knew it–I was face down in the North Dakota dirt with each fist around a sunflower stalk, holding on as I had in Blackstone just before Appomattox. I consciously could smell the dirt and the sweet smells the morning made when dew was strong. But this time I could control the color of the fog in the air; I wanted brown, the love and home on Karen's chart. And I wanted Vicky Derryberry to be there with Harvey, my sensitive side in my novel 'The Paper Man'. Could I will what I wanted? Could I see any thing or person I needed to, in order for a resolution in a past life? Could I please be here with Vee when I get to my feet, and not with my dead brother, not with Grant or Lee or any of their dead and wounded that I saw in the Wilderness?

I had to find her, take her with me, so I reached for her, for those perfect legs but found her ankles just before the spin became the swift whirling motion that could send me to God knows where.

All winter long I had been out of this vortex, telling Karen to only send me to green places on my chart, to the libraries where I would find prosperity by selling copies of 'Shy Ann' like gang-busters. And I would not even know how my book was received in these places unless I asked. I never asked. I didn't want to know. Because this very moment to be with Vee would perhaps be ruined if I was told the book was good or bad. If it was good: I may send it to publishers so they would market my books for me; and a publisher may say they will take it on if only I stop selling it myself.

If it was bad: I might move to Canada where voices are diminished tenfold in the same amount of space.

But then: the brown haze vanished along with other vicissitudes. My hands. They were smaller. Dirt was caked under all my fingernails. My glasses felt heavy on my nose. I removed them to rub my sore ears. They were black glasses like Buddy Holly wore in the 50s. My legs and arms and feet were the size they were when I was a boy of nine or ten.

I got up onto my feet fast. But now I was in a field of corn and my hay fever was back. I looked around and thought it must be summer. Then I looked around for Vee with the racing heart of a boy in trouble. No Vee. Was it me? I had to see my face, so I began running down the dirt road that I thought was in the same direction that would lead me back to Traveller.

On and on I ran, until rounding a bend that stopped my legs from moving. The only sounds were those of summer insects and birds so alive in the dense wooded area ahead that looked so familiar to me. I knew this was not North Dakota where only one percent of the entire state is forested. And then I saw the park entrance I knew so well in my boyhood.

—Ledges, I whispered.

The sign that used to be located here was gone, yet I knew this had to be the same place that my character Ben in 'Ledges' loved to escape to. Then it hit me: Ben..I was Ben the city boy whose mother married the abusive farmer Dutch in 'Ledges' my second novel.

I had to see my face. I ran toward the park's restrooms, but there were no mirrors above the sinks. I tried to see my image in the aluminum paper towel dispenser, but it was too distorted to make out any definite features. Before I darted out of the restroom–I had to eliminate. Whoever I was, Ben or myself, I sat on the hopper with my belly still full from the big breakfast I had with Vee just a short while ago in North Dakota. And then it scared me to see that my unit was the same one I always had. I must be me, I knew.

After my elimination I washed my hands with a palmful of

Borax from the dispenser. Before I left the restroom I was not sure I would still be in Ledges State Park. I was. There were no clues to tell me what year it is; there were no people around or any vehicles. My tennis shoes, shorts and T-shirt could be from any era within the last fifty years. I took the road that I knew would lead to the heart of the park, conscious of the giant oak trees all around the narrow winding road in the darkest shade of the park.

A blue jay flew across my path some twenty feet away; it appeared to pause in flight to wink at me, giving me this creepy feeling that the deeper I walked into the park–the cooler it became, like I was being sealed in this sarcophagus and this place was my tomb. Did this mean that my book 'Ledges' had captured me and taken my life somewhere I was not destined to go? I wondered. But then I relaxed, by telling myself that after I see what I'm supposed to see–I'll return to the present..and write up a storm about what I experienced here.

A storm. That's what was coming. I had written about it in 'Ledges'. A terrible storm deluged Ledges, trapping Karen. Karen. Only my family knew that Karen was the character Pam in 'Ledges'. And Karen was mad at first for me writing about her unflattering flatulations throughout the story, and the ordeal when the evil Hutch character fondled her. They were both true, but Karen didn't want the world to know it.

The sky over Ledges was never like this in my book: yellow with swirling streaks of black. From Karen's chart I recalled that yellow meant family/past lives and black represents mind. As I reached the curve that brought into view the heart of the park where on my right the park opened up with the sandstone ledges most prominently. My eyes looked up high to Inspiration Point, the place where Ben found Pam during the storm. It was atop Inspiration Point where best friends Gene and D. J. used to go in 'Ledges', the same 'High Place' where D. J. jumped to his death.

It began to rain hard only around this part of the park, like when you're standing at the edge of the rainfall; this spot was that edge. And it wasn't moving. Then I could see somebody up there at the highest point in Ledges. My heart started racing again with my legs, faster and faster until I reached the wide railroad timber steps that led to the top. I worried if it was my brother, my best friend up there and if I could stop him from killing himself. As my legs ached more and more I thought it might be Karen who fell from a cliff like this when she was young. She had slipped and rolled all the way down to the bottom with dirt clods lodged in her teeth with her spine severely damaged. Either way, I wanted this to be a rescue and not a terrible loss I'd already endured over my brother's death. Nearing the top:

     —JOHNNY! KAREN! I'M HERE! IT'S DWAYNE!

     Just then: the rain stopped. The park was still again. The sun was coming out and blinding me. I knew now that I was Dwayne the boy with all my adult memories. At the top I saw the back of a young girl with short blonde hair who was about my age. Her back was to me as she sat with her legs dangling over the top ledge. I wondered why she hadn't turned back to see me when I called out. When she did turn to me I could see those hazel eyes of Vicky Derryberry just as big and penetrating as they were in Minot. She had a missing front tooth, behind a half-smile that had been recently hurt and had given up trusting adults.

     I sat beside her as Gene had done with D. J. in 'Ledges'. As I focused on the green treetops that now splayed out to the blue horizon, I could feel those eyes on me, sizing me up to see if she could trust me. I said softly to the vista in a boy's voice:

     —Do you remember me?

     —Yes, she said with an adorable lisp. I met you at Eddie's in Minot. We were in a field of sunflowers..and now we're here.
I turned my blonde head to hers and could see that she is frightened. I said:

     —It's okay to be scared..but I've been here before..and this has happened to me a few times.

     —Is this because of your sister's chart?

     —Yes, somehow all these places she sends me to have a way of making my life worth living. Before..I was half dead. Now I'm looking forward to it all. She never sends me to places I can't handle.

—How long will we be here?

—I don't know. Usually it goes away after I've seen some thing or person I need to. I really don't know.

—Will you stay with me until we go back?

—Yes.

I noticed her tiny fingers tremble on the broken clod of shale beside her tan bare knee, a knee that was dry and scratched as if she'd recently fallen. Never as a boy would I have taken her hand in mine; that would be too far removed from who I used to be. But now..I did. She liked it, because there was no bad energy about it. It wasn't like the ugly things done to her by her stepfather. For both of us, we had seen the negative world of dysfunctional adults who have no business raising children in what should be the golden innocence of youth.

Then it hit me: I was not here for just myself; I was here for Vee, for little Vicky Derryberry. All I knew was that I had to get her away from this place, where D. J. ended his life in 'Ledges'.

—I want to show you a nice place in the park.

—You've been here before?

—Yes..it's a place in my second book 'Ledges'.

As I helped her to her feet with my strong left hand she asked me why she is here.

—I don't know.

We held hands all the way down to the paved two-way lane that was now filling with people and traffic. Children and adults were playing in the cold rock bed streams that overflowed in places on the road. Our arms and legs were light with no tension as before; it felt good not to have any connection to other people here, or to have to return to a home we did not want to return to.

When we stopped to soak our bare feet in the stream she asked me if I knew now that I wanted to be a writer.

—No, I said.

—I did...when I was six, she said.

—How old are you now?

—I don't know, she said.

—Me neither.

We carried our shoes and began laughing while we skipped down the lane all the way to the back entrance to the park. I knew right where to go to find the most beautiful part of the park via a narrow dirt trail that led to the place I wanted her to see, a route where the color green was most dominant. Green was all over the trees and on the lush vegetation that was so alive with a thousand species of birds and insects, making the park so thrilling to be in.

I took her hand again, so she stayed on my heels on the narrow trail. I so wanted her to see every bird's nest and knothole, and there: that birdhouse for the owls made of gray barnwood a hundred feet high and appeared to be suspended from the sky. The energy was so connected between us, she seemed to see just what I wanted her to see with my back to her. I became so excited I walked backwards, pulling her gently, wanting to see all the wonder and awe on her face as I talked fast to her, yet keeping my head turned left and right in order to stay on the trail:

—We are right here, Vee! Now! There's nothing in the whole world to distract us! Isn't it wonderful?
She nodded yes and, unselfconscious about the gap between her teeth, smiling so big and beautiful, I had to stop and put both my hands on her frail shoulders and said:

—That's the first time I've seen you really smile, Vee! Do it more please! It looks so good on you!

I kept smiling with my back to her as she continued to follow me along the trail without my hand. I began to narrate like a park ranger:

—This is my millionth time in Ledges..except when I was here in my mind while writing about it. This place has its own ecosystem..and was formed by a glacier some sixty thousand years ago. It floods here about every six years.

—You sound like a writer.
I laughed, then she continued:

—My mother tells me that children who create..will not destroy.
I repeated her words so I could remember them:

—Children who create..will not destroy. I like that. If I

was a writer I'd say that. Vee, you sound like a writer.

—I write things, she said, but I tear them up.

I found myself smiling from her lisp, the same one little Josie had in my book 'The Paper Man'. I wanted to tell her about it, but instead I asked her why she tears up her writing.

—Because it would hurt my mom.

I waited for her to continue as we reached a small bridge made from park timber that spanned a pool of water only inches deep; this is the same spot in 'Ledges' where Ben and Pam saw a deer and Ben compared the deer to Gene their bus driver.

I stopped on the bridge, leaning against the rail; Vee did likewise on the other rail across from me eight feet away.

—Look! A turtle! I exclaimed.

She came over to stand next to me and see the turtle:

—Where?

She looked in the direction of his pointing finger and watched the turtle inching along the muddy shore of the pond when I asked her why it would hurt her mom and she answered me with her eyes yet on the turtle:

—Children who create..will not destroy.

—You said that. What do you mean? I smiled.

—If I write about my life with my mom and stepdad..and how bad he is to me.. I mean..if I write this story from my heart..it would kill my mother. Children who create..

—..will not destroy. I understand. Maybe when you're older you'll write about that stuff.

She said nothing more about it. Like that turtle now hiding in the mud, I could see she was going into her shell, that place that I had known so well when I lived near here.

I couldn't help her. I wasn't trained for that. I could only understand her, and that is all anyone really wants. And I thought it strange that I was just as sad as Vee in my heart when I was this age, but not now. Never did I feel this good when I was a boy. Then I remembered something my sister E-mailed me from the library. She said that we all create mental picture, which are thoughts of other people in our lives. These thoughts stick in our bodies and envelop in the layers of the aura–the space around us. We also adjust ourselves and our thought patterns to match those around us. We become programmed or conditioned to act in a specific manner. When you end a relationship you undo this type of conditioning. Two people deposit positive or negative pictures of who the other person is on the edge of the aura. It is important to release both types because these thought patterns act as a doorway for that person's energy to come back into your space. And Karen's words in that E-mail were with me now, along with her words on the phone when I was at a signing in Wisconsin last winter: "Energy is not good or bad. It's either yours or someone elses."

I took Vee's hand again and led her off the trail, uphill, along an obscure ridge of scattered rocks and weeds, and this panoply of dozens of diverse trees clustered together as only in Ledges State Park. There it was: Flat Rock, the panoramic 40-foot-high perch where Ben and Pam came to see the river flowing past the fertile land. I told Vee to close her eyes as I guided her onto the granite stone that was 20 times older than man. I whispered to her with her eyes closed:

—Vee, don't open your eyes yet.

I positioned myself in front of her in case she peeked. I could feel her peeking but closed them fast when she saw that my eyes were closed behind my lenses. Then I peeked at her and could see that she trusted me and squeezed her eyes shut. We could feel the humid breeze coming from the west had been cooled; it was charged with this swift/powerful energy from a million acres of rich earth that will yield millions of bushels of corn and soy beans. Yes, this was my land, farmed by my people, the Dutch and Germans and Irish and Swedes. And without the loss of my brother I would not be here now, with Vee, the waitress I found in Minot because of my need to escape the terrible loss of my brother.

I took her tiny hands in mine and held them tight, for this is the way I want to remember her. The writer, the creator of books, I will have this moment be the way I want it to be. But she would be the one to live forever, on the pages of my book. For I knew young Vicky Derryberry was right. I could truly never be the good writer I had inside me, because I only write fiction, about the dead and imagined, about the way of lies told in words that will never mean squat in reality, except for my readers who want to get lost with me in all my books, just to find out how important it is to open our eyes together and see that I can be trusted.

With our eyes closed on Flat Rock I was now the man I was in North Dakota. With my adult voice I told young Vicky that she had to read 'Ledges' to understand the courage it took for Ben to place his head on Gene's heart and feel the salty tears of real love that ran down the back of Ben's ear and to the trailer floor. Just as now, when young Vicky opened her eyes and saw Dwayne Dayne, the man who she trusted enough to fall into my chest and stay pressed to my heart as I held her. She began to cry for forgiveness just as Darlene had in 'Ledges'.

She kept crying under the now-yellow sky of Ledges, letting go more and more until she finished riding this storm of violent poundings with her fists onto my chest, each one sending my heart more and more compassion. I knew this was her time for a breakthrough, an emotional letting go in order that Vee, the woman, could truly be with me now. We knelt embracing with our eyes closed again, unaware that we were so close to the edge of Flat Rock. We believed that if we fell, together, we would not be afraid.

I could feel her body changing back into Vee the woman. I opened my eyes when she did, and now on Flat Rock I was with Vee, the beautiful woman I met in Minot. We could see a brown mist of odorless smoke or fog coming toward us from the river far below where we could now see Traveller parked across the river, our home, just as Karen's chart had said.

Now, if I could trust her, I could have the woman of my dreams in a maddening world that separates lovers. Our home was so close, just across the river; we could see it within our reach..if we could just fall together..now..when the wind from the east held back..waiting..until it came: the same sound Harvey chose in my novel 'The Paper Man'; it was coming from Traveller, the Boz

Scaggs song 'Heart of Mine' had begun at the edge of lost in love in our liquid light of hazel and blue.

She accepted that energy that had sustained me for a million miles, alone, on back roads that led to ten thousand cities and towns. And I was lost in those two circles of green/gold/blue that were so ripe with health, spirit and prosperity that were now mine. It was then that I lost all sense of fear and rolled west with her in my arms..into the music..so confident that Traveller would catch us unharmed. We fell into the brown aberration, into the lyrics, she held on with her legs around me and her arms around my neck..falling..falling..until I found the lost girl. She knew that she had lost her will to trust, but now she was turning into something new that I hoped I was emotionally mature enough to handle. Because what I really loved about Vee was that unaccommodating, unyielding hardness of a girl stuck, even after having the courage to emotionally escape from her parents, a letting–go thing she had done when young.

As 'Heart of Mine' continued to play, we knew we had landed and safely, with our eyes closed, and together in this torpid caress below the yellow sunflowers. When the music faded out, all we could hear, just above us, was the prairie wind making the soft fluttering sounds of the stems and stalks in motion.

We opened our eyes together, knowing now that we loved each other, and that what we just experienced had to be related to Karen's chart. Vee brushed away flecks of soil stuck to my cheeks and I knew now that I had my gold wire-rimmed glasses back, for she straightened them for me. We sat up, the sunflowers still above us. I took her hand and told her about the times this had happened to me and that I believed she came along because I held onto her just as the spinning began.

At first she thought the cook in the café where we had breakfast had laced our food with peyote. I felt different. Alive. I stood, taking her hand with me. We started out of the field in a hurry with me leading her by the hand. I knew what I wanted to do next. And she was pushing me in the same direction with this incredible energy that love gives to a man who has lived without it for so long.

On the walk back to Traveller on that dirt road that turned to pavement we talked excitedly about what we saw in Ledges.

—The feel of that place was incredible, she said.

—I must've wanted you to go there with me. To return to Ledges with you was something I wanted but something you needed.

—I feel lighter, she laughed.

—Me, too. Look, to hell with that left-handed town. It doesn't seem to interest me now. Let's go south to the Badlands. I want to be with you in the Black Hills.

—Whatever, she laughed.

—That's an impulsive thing I want to do. Are you sure you want to go there with me?

Lost and Found

For only 20 miles we went west on 50 before dropping south on 8 for 50 miles until we reached the Missouri River at its widest point. As Vee sat up front with her legs extended comfortably on the dash, her Sheryl Crow CD blaring, that dreaded pain in my groin was back; I hadn't experienced that discomfort so intensely since I was in my roaring 20s.

I thought Sheryl would never shut up. She played the entire CD twice, until the beginning of the Dakota Badlands started to cover all of Traveller's glass. We had picked up 22 south for a hundred miles until we cruised into Dickinson, North Dakota where it was time to refuel.

It was four hours later when we crossed into South Dakota, a place in the state where neither of us had ever been before. It was back at a truck stop where 22 turned to 79 that I saw Vee bum a smoke from a trucker and hotbox it near his cab. That's when I noticed the colors on the horizon had changed to a yellow violet and decided to call Karen before the sunset. I called her at home from my cell phone when Vee returned from having her quick smoke. I had Vee give my sister all the info she would need to do her chart. I had told my sister that we would camp for the night in the Custer National Forest and Karen quickly read my chart and said it was a good place for me to be. A good sign.

Karen told Vee it would take her a few days before she finished her chart because she was working on a deadline to finish a grant for a library on an Arizona reservation. I could tell Karen felt better about Vee after making fun of my quest to become this writer/in.

I overheard that Vee's 32, born in 1970, when I was a freshman in junior high. That didn't sound too bad to me. At least I wasn't old enough to be her father..in most states. Victoria Elizabeth Derryberry didn't know her exact time of birth, yet she was sure it was close to midnight on the 4th of February in Glendale, California. Karen told Vee that it was close enough since Vee remembered her mother telling her that it was real close to midnight.

As Vee laughed at my sister's snide humor, I could see the Custer National Forest an hour beyond Traveller's windshield. I really wanted to camp there in the forest or near it, for I wanted it to be a romantic setting..I hoped. Of course, I would let music set the mood for romance. This was going to be a memorable night, straight from the pages of 'The Paper Man'. Yes, the creator of Harvey Deason finally had his Josie, and not some imaginary character who lived on his pages and followed a storyline. This was real and good. Big difference.

We would camp in the forest in a designated area for RVs and campers. A half-dozen motor homes were spaced 50 feet apart between yellow parking lines that terraced uphill with no electrical hookup service provided. That's okay because Traveller has his own generator.

Our neighbors were friendly yet not too friendly, maintaining a comfortable distance–except for the men, their eyeballs I could see were taking in Vee in her frayed cut-off jeans and belly shirt while she danced outside Traveller to another Sheryl Crow CD. This was an important test for me. I had trouble trusting any woman to be loyal to just me in the past. Especially a girl that every man wanted. I knew that would be one of my great lessons to learn and resolve; it was right up there with the loss of my brother John.

I watched that beautiful girl dance, lost in her music, her hips moving in figure 8s on an imaginary timeline: she was standing right on the spot where the Central Standard Time Zone met Mountain. I saw this invisible line mapped out on a historical marker behind glass twenty yards from where we parked. Custer National Forest ran west into Montana some 40 miles from here.

When I returned to Traveller Vee was still dancing to Sheryl; I danced with her for only a few seconds before going inside my home. Soon, she came in, wanting to go with me on a long walk. She put on walking shoes while sitting on my queen-sized bed that I had named Lucky last winter. I had never gotten lucky on Lucky yet; the closest I got to lucky was with Ann from Asheville.

My spirit rose in more ways than one when Vee laid back spread-eagle on Lucky with her shoes hanging over the end of the bed when she said to me:

—I'll bet I sleep great here.

I don't think she saw my eyes widen when I heard that, or saw the smirk on my mouth when I imagined being with her, getting lucky on Lucky.

When Vee ducked into the bathroom I thought about one night this last winter near Madison, Wisconsin in a town called Black Earth. My three titles were popular there. At a library signing there, this middle-aged woman with red hair and too much jewelry for her 40-something years, gave me a sealed, perfume-scented pink envelope after I signed to her a copy of 'Shy Ann'. Pink was the same color Karen had told me was running straight through Black Earth. Passion/career represents pink on my chart. After the woman left, I opened the envelope, and on this piece of pink paper were the ominous printed words: "If you lie..you fry. And I smell smoke."

I smiled at the memory, recalling how I woke up several times that night on Lucky, paranoid about smelling smoke from a fire set by some looney reader. I told myself that I think I remembered that message in Black Earth because I had seen her smoking with that trucker.

We left Traveller with little light left in the day. We walked west into a westerly dry wind. The trees were mostly pine with drooping boughs from the last heavy snowfall, right in the middle of the Dakota Badlands, a place where Custer and his men camped before the Little Big Horn. Vee led the way on a trail when she confessed:

—I broke down and smoked a cigarette today.

—So..begin again..or..forgive yourself and have another one.

Vee laughed loud, the first time I'd heard her true laugh, a sound that said she trusted me.

—You seem chilled about it, she laughed.

—It used to be 'cool' in the 50s and 60s. Now it's 'chilled'..but this place is cool.

—Yes, it is cool.

—Just think, Vee..if you ever fall for me..you'd have two perfect asses..yours..and me.

—That's funny, she laughed.

Again it was her uninhibited laugh, kind of goofy but real and so attractive to me.

It was when a red Labrador trotted past us in an area clogged with Canadian RVers on bicycles, she told me about her dream to be an actress. I told her I had gone to the same acting studio when I lived there.

—How long ago was that? she asked.

—I don't know. I'm not good at remembering years. Maybe it was seven or eight years ago..maybe ten..I don't remember. So, you were a pretty good actor, huh?

—I was good. Yeah. I think I could've made it.

—Remember that one exercise when you'd get up on that dark stage with a light on you with the class right there in front of you on folding chairs..and you'd have to sing and dance while focusing on someone in the audience..and then look at the face of the next person and so on while changing dance styles?

—Yeah..and you'd project on each face differently. That was wild. It was all about movement and seeing what you reflect..and finding out where you hold tension in your body.

—Yes..and some of the faces were petrified..and that fear could get into your body if you let it. It was all so incredibly hard and dangerous..and interesting as hell.

—I miss it.

—Then go back to it, I said.

—I don't know.

—Yeah, you're getting divorced and now's not the time to commit to a tough thing like that. You gotta be really able to handle rejection. It's a tough business. If you're not totally dedicated to it..you end up like a hundred thousand other wannabes in L.A.

—That's just it..you have to live in L.A. to break into film. My family's there. I got married to get away from them. And I have no desire to be around them at all.

—Then live in San Diego or Ventura and go into L.A. for auditions and showcases. You don't have to live there.

—Yeah.

She stopped on the trail. I went past her, brushing her waist with my fingertips, knowing she wanted me to lead now. She wanted to be able to look at the colors around her more intensely, to see the birds flitting here and there from branch to branch, from tree to tree, and, most of all–to really listen to an older voice, a man who could lead her now. She was tired of dragging Butch around by his ear, telling him what to do, even how to make love to her.

She walked and watched and listened to her new friend and fellow actor, willing to be taken wherever he led her, if he could prove to her that she could fall..and return to him. It was becoming clear to her in this light remaining after a summer sunset, between all the million clingings of shuddering chartreuse leaves hanging above them as they walked by. Yes, she knew that Vicky Derryberry was released too young, way before she was ready to let go of her real father. She even knew it was yet there when Butch told her to call him Big Daddy when they made love.

Paul Derryberry, Vee's father, the senior machinist foreman at the Long Beach Naval Shipyard was never there emotionally or unconditionally for his only child. She knew early on that her father would quit having kids if the first one was a girl. His father and brother each had five girls, and plenty of troubles raising them. No way was Paul going to repeat that pattern. So, he worked seven nights a week and slept all day while young Vicky played quietly alone or far enough from the house so her father could get his rest. But she blamed her mother for not playing with her, or for not getting her to socialize more. Until she started dating young, lots of boys. Until her father noticed or said something. He never did.

Somehow, after expressing her dream to be an actress, and her thoughts about her parents and lonely girlhood, they did not feel like they bothered her as an issue to resolve now. She wondered if this had something to do with visiting Ledges with this man leading her now. Just then: on their right in an open meadow, this burnt orange bed of sunflowers appeared in one movement to droop like old celery inside a weathered tractor tire.

I followed her over to the tire and stood squinting into the tip of sunset, looking at the stagnant rusty rainwater pooled in the tire's rubber rim. I watched her bend her knees to the earth and palm out some water from the rim, and with this gentle flick that contradicted her tough-chick image, she hit the tops of every limp sunflower bud. When she stepped inside the black rubber circle we witnessed it together. Each stalk moved, and began to wave without a trace of wind. Each orange bud appeared to lean toward her and open wider as any hungry thing. I noticed that even a few lower that had not received her offering were leaning in her direction.

I stooped down onto my haunches as if I were some patient hound waiting for and watching someone I loved. Her eyes came up, up, to mine. They were no longer hazel; they had turned to the same yellow/gold eyes of Josephine in 'The Paper Man'. And I could see love in each eye, as those dark orange sunflowers loved her for these moments–unconditionally.

She could see that he loved her, too, for she knew well that real love cannot be one sided, that it takes two to see it in the other. But they were only seeing what they were showing at this moment, both knowing it will not last long or be something they can see at will any other time. Their skulls tingled from the waves of electricity a man and a woman generate when she makes him feel young again. It was there again, this power that was always there yet never used. She was offering to take the boy back, to her safe place, as he had taken little Vicky to Ledges. If only he would touch the palm of her outstretched left hand, this rough hand of a waitress who wrote in this safe place so long ago.

Her hand yet held drops of that magic water that had made

sunflowers dance openly in this isolated part of the Custer National Forest, at sunset on this imaginary timeline where there was no time..if I'd only take her hand. After I, too, stepped inside the tire it was my left hand that reached for hers, above the dancing sunflowers that were now turning yellow.

Just when we touched hands the tire began to spin around us counterclockwise in the same yellow haze I saw in Virginia. I knew well that yellow meant family/past lives. But this was Vee's spin, to her place, the place where she first discovered the incredible power of feminine energy.

She knew they had to be headed to L.A. because that's all she knew. Just as Dwayne had to take her to Ledges, a place where his story was safe, she had to go back to Culver City, a middle class oasis south of Beverly Hills and home of Sony Studios now. This was where her dream to become an actress began and the power of feminine energy discovered.

When she opened her eyes she was also in a park. It was one of a hundred small city parks in the L.A. area that covers only one square block, shaded with massive oak and elm and the solid white birch. There were no palm trees back here. Palmettos were for the tourists on Washington Avenue three blocks away and lining both sides of the avenue for a hundred city blocks.

This was the same city park two blocks from their cottage, where she and her parents lived for the first seven years of her life; and it was the park where she had her boyfriend Butch drive her to when they first made love on the tattered seat of his old Dodge pickup. Back then, it was an attempt to bring balanced harmony to a shattered mind, and heal it forever by getting the hell outta Dodge.

As Dwayne did in Ledges, she looked at her arms and legs to gauge her age; and she wanted to see her face. She thought she was around 24 years old. She had never looked better physically, yet she felt that familiar emptiness from wanting to be a famous actress in order to be happy.

The sun could not penetrate the usual haze though it was late afternoon, yet sometimes the haze would be burned away by now, she knew. Not far off she saw a cluster of little purple ground cover flowers she knew to be Trailing Blue Lobelias, her favorites. She went over to them and knelt, pulling just one from the earth. She twirled its magenta stem near her nose and could not smell any fragrance except that familiar metallic sting of smog that soaked into everything above the earth.

This was her first neighborhood when a little girl. She looked around at the clean homes that were all different in shape, size and landscaping. As at Ledges when she first arrived, there was no sign of another person in sight. She walked east, in the direction of her old cottage that a retired school teacher rented to her parents. The teacher lived in a large house in front of the cottage. Vee could not remember their landlord's name but remembered she had a small swimming pool and that the old lady was friendly, always waving hello to little Vicky.

When Vee came to her old street and had to turn right in order to go to the cottage, instead she went left and began to run. She was running to him. To her safe place, where she would dream about becoming the most famous actress the world has ever known.

She stopped running at Washington Avenue in front of Sony Studios. A black iron fence bordered the imposing studio lot. She turned right, heading east, again on the run, until she saw it: her safe place. She stopped moving, breathing hard, looking at it with her back to the studio.

It was the Culver Hotel. A famous nightclub used to be on the old hotel's ground floor. The hotel was shaped like no other building she'd ever seen. Like a six-story wedge that tapered to this narrow side, two rooms wide, made of early 20th Century brick mortared from Chatsworth. The hotel widened at the other end, six rooms wide, with Washington Avenue split around each side. John Wayne and Red Skelton owned the hotel at different times, she was told by her father. And what a Hollywood history the hotel has. It's where the cast of 'Wizard of Oz' stayed while filming at another nearby studio to the east.

Vee began to walk toward it recalling all those remarkable black and white photos she'd studied on the walls on every floor of that hotel. But then she noticed the stem of the tiny purple flower was yet in her hand, but now the once brilliant flower had closed to a shriveled death. How fast it died, she thought.

At the northeast corner of the historic hotel there was this darker shade of brick that never received direct sunlight. Vee paused before stepping under the Kelly green canvas awning above the hotel's lobby entrance. Her hazel eyes went to the top floor to the southeast corner room window that was open. How do I know that's his room? she asked herself. Before opening the shaded glass door she froze upon seeing her reflection. She was Vee at 24, so it must be around 1994, about the time she got her first tatoo, a red heart about the size of a quarter below her belly button just above her pubic hair.

Inside the lobby she went up the wide marble stairs and was not seen by the desk clerk on the phone. Halfway up to the narrow third floor she stopped to unbutton her pants to see if she had her red heart tattoo. It was there; it looked new, a rich red. Never before had she chased a boy or a man; she always let them show interest and pursue her. Except for Butch. And look how that turned out, she reminded herself.

Upon reaching the top floor, six, she slowed her step, for her breath was labored and magnified in the quiet hallway. The carpet was a plush maroon and welcome after the sidewalks of Culver City. Down the length of the hallway she stopped at each of the sixteen black and white photos on the wall to her right. They were production stills taken in the late 30s on the set of 'The Wizard of Oz'. When she was the seven-year-old Vicky Derryberry she'd sneak into one of the open rooms when one of the Mexican maids was cleaning. Beliz was on the maid's nametag, she remembered. They never spoke the first half-dozen times or so, yet the friendly maid would smile every time they saw each other in the hallway. One day, when Beliz was cleaning room 611, the room he lived in now, she excitedly told the little girl a story about room 611. The maid said how this room was one of the rooms the famous Munchkins stayed in while filming 'Oz'; and she told me how the little Munchkins slept three across lengthwise on one bed.

Beliz went on to say how the Munchkins got sick eating pistachio ice cream, and that only a few months ago one of the hotel residents on the sixth floor complained to the manager that she believed her room was haunted because all the pistachios were missing in her half-gallon of pistachio ice cream.

That was all little Vicky needed to hear. From then on she would scour the old hotel as if it were her private sanctuary filled with friendly little ghosts; it was as if she were Dorothy the actress and this was her Emerald City.

Now: this was the time to knock on the corner room door of 611, his door, as he had done in Minot at Eddie's hotel. She didn't know what day of the week it was or even what year. All she was certain of is that this is his room, the actor, the writer, the older man who had studied at the same actor's studio where she had. That this stranger who took her to that Iowa park and held her and rescued her by getting her out of Minot. This same man had lived here..now..some 17 years after she was lost here.

This metaphysical chart his sister created had somehow brought her to this polished mahogany door to 611 that she now softly knocked on. She stepped back as she felt his eyes staring at her from his peephole. When he opened his door smiling, she could see that he was eight years younger with a bit more hair on his head. There was something different about him; he appeared anxious about something when he said her name 'Vee'. His pale blue eyes looked healthy and bigger behind his copper-framed lenses. He pulled her inside the room quickly and kissed her with her back pressed against his closed door. They continued kissing with their hands all over each other until he walked Vee over to the bed and they fell together, passionate for each other, rolling and kissing and raising her shirt above her small breasts, kissing them until he discovered her heart and kissed that, too. She had never stopped a lover before now. Why now? he asked.

—I don't know. I'm supposed to be here with you now, but not jump right into the sack. I used to come here to this room when I was a little girl.

—To this room?

—To the hotel. I lived a few blocks from here. I want to show you where I lived.

Vee bounced off the bed pulling down her top and buttoning her pants. She noticed a page in his typewriter and went over to it.

—What are you working on?

—My script 'The Paper Man'.

—What's it about?

He stayed on the bed with his hands clasped behind his head, enthralled and in pain from her beauty.

—It's about a Midwest toilet paper salesman. He's an older man who falls in love with a girl..about your age.

—Does she love him?

—I think so, he smiled.

She blushed, knowing he was flirting with her.

—Are you the Paper Man?

—You'll have to read it to find out.

—Is it your first screenplay?

—I've written several. From my novels.

—I'd like to read the novel when we get back.

—I've got one in Traveller's glove box. I signed it to you the day I saw you in the Minot beauty shop..when you bought 'Shy Ann'.

—I noticed that the cover to 'Shy Ann' doesn't stay closed like a quality book.

—I know..it's like my printer put Viagra on it.

—Viagra? she laughed.

—Yeah, that's what I'll tell my librarians if they mention it when I try to sell 'em my next book. My printer made a mistake and left out this nylon chemical that makes covers stay flat. Half are printed with Viagra and half without. That's part of the hassle with self-publishing. You have to live with other people's mistakes. If that idiot who f....d up my book had to sell every one of 'em to my libraries like I have to..he prob'ly would've done it right the first time.

On their walk through Culver City they held hands. He told

her how he lived in that room eight years ago, and that he moved out right after the Northridge earthquake. He explained how he was the first one out of the building when the old hotel started to shake, even though he was stopped in the stairway by a woman in her underwear who asked him for a pair of pants.

—So I ran back up to my room, grabbed my long underwear, gave them to her and ran down the six flights before anyone else was outside. When I first opened the front entrance door to the hotel I saw some old bricks that had shaken loose from the elevator shaft and landed right where I might've been if that woman hadn't stopped me for some pants.

And Vee had a good laugh when he told her that he never got his longjohns back because the woman was having her period at that time, and that her time of the month might've just saved his life.

Then it dawned on Vee that this must be about the same time when the Northridge quake happened.

—Where were you during the quake? he asked.

—I was in a motel in Ventura.

It was a longshot coincidence to Dwayne that his brother John was also in a Ventura motel the night of the earthquake.

They continued walking along the pleasant residential street, so clean and middle class, and filled with memories for the girl Vicky Derryberry. When she pointed to her old white cottage, Dwayne was flashing back to moments just days before the Northridge quake:

It was a few blocks west of the Culver Hotel on a concrete pedestrian island that offered the most panoramic view and best angle of the hotel. John had spent the night in his brother's room, sharing the same queen-sized bed that once crammed in three or four Munchkins.

Dwayne spoke out loud as Vee stood staring at the front wall of the cottage that was her childhood home:

—I want to show you something.

She walked with him back toward Washington Avenue. No

words were said between them. Vee had thought until now that this return to Culver City was for her alone. Now she knew that this is for both of them. He told her that he had lived in the same cottage right after the quake when he moved out of the hotel. He said he lived there for six months, and described the interior of her old home just the way she remembered it.

—That's no coincidence, she told him.

He chose not to ask questions about the night in the Ventura motel. There were lots of motels there. It didn't matter to him now. Only that they were here now because of the chart his sister created.

They crossed Washington Avenue with no traffic in either direction. Dwayne stopped to gauge the very spot where he was standing when he saw his brother staring aloofly at the hotel. He pointed for Vee to look at the narrow end of the hotel's wedge as he recalled what he saw while standing here with his brother:

—I had a long minute to study him. Never had I looked so long and hard at a person I loved. I could see that he was not himself. But I didn't know what to do for him. I remember his bald head was bare and his face had a pale ruddiness from too much bad sleep. His tongue would roll behind his lips as he stood mesmerized here by the hotel..with those big cornflower blue eyes that were glazed wide from some kind of chemical imbalance. If you knew him then..he would have told you he was touring country/western concerts. He would travel all over Texas and Wyoming and Colorado..covering thousands of miles in his T-bird. He called himself J.D. when he worked on the oil rigs off the coast near Ventura. He was so lost when he came here. For that minute..he was a lost boy in a 250-pound body. I'll never forget the anguish I saw on his face. He was completely unaware I was with him.

When Dwayne turned to her he said:

—I don't want to know or need to know anything about your past. We were put together so we can become free from something I don't yet understand. Maybe it's about forgiveness of the past. It's all so strange, isn't it?

She nodded yes.

They stood together looking at the hotel. He decided not to tell her about his brother's death, for he had been down that road too many times. Guilt, grief and terrible sadness were always there if he ignored forgiveness. Now, he had to have more fun in his life.

When her left hand felt the squeeze from his left hand, letting her know that all is well between them, and just when she looked into those eyes of forgiveness: the clockwise spin began with Culver City circling them until:

The sun had set in the forest around us. We stood together beside the old tractor tire that surrounded the sunflowers. We were back in the present. As at Ledges State Park, everything that we experienced in Culver City we could remember as if it had just happened.

On our slow walk back to Traveller we said nothing until we neared some of the other vehicles parked near Traveller:

—I want a cigarette, she confessed.

—I could go for a smoke, too. There's a store we passed a few miles back. I'll take Lawn Boy.

—Your car?

—Yeah.

She laughed and said:

—You name everything, don't you?

—Some things. Not everything. I think I name them because I live alone. It makes my life more real. I talk to them when I'm alone..sometimes..for company I s'pose.

After backing Lawn Boy off the trailer I grabbed a CD from Traveller's cab. On the way to the store we listened to 'Heart of Mine' by Boz Scaggs, both of us yet remote from our visit to Culver City. Halfway into the song I reached for her hand and she took it as if she were beginning to love me. I could feel her fingers rubbing my smooth hand with a warm tenderness that I knew had been foreign to her during her marriage.

Was it all real? she asked herself as the song was winding down when he parked in front of the old convenience store.

That's when I leaned over to kiss her. She stayed with my kiss; it tasted like the kissing in room 611.

Vee bought a pack of American Spirit ultra lights; we smoked near Lawn Boy in front of the faded green and white store that used to be a Sinclair gas station.

—Last fall I would spin back to the Civil War era..alone in The Wilderness..or my brother and I would show up as Grant and Lee at Appomattox. Then, all winter..no spinning back..until now, with you.

—Your sister said it's because of the chemistry of our combined astrological signs..and the places we happen to be together.

—I believe it's connected to my brother's death..somehow.

—He died?

—Yeah..and because you knew him maybe in a past life..you are able to take these spins or regressions with me.

—Or maybe you're supposed to write about them..to become a better writer.

—I think about that. I wrote about it in 'Shy Ann'. The main thing for me is that it gives me a much more interesting life to live and write about. Before, when I was not using this chart, my life was so dull. I thought I was headed for some isolated grain elevator out here..where I'd work alone in the middle of nowhere. And live in some dinky prairie town that wasn't even on a map.

—Are you afraid of being a successful writer?

—No..because I am a successful writer. I do well just writing and selling my books without a real job.

—That is successful. I want to read 'The Paper Man'.

I flicked my cigarette to the ground:

—Look, something is bothering me. Were you with a big bald guy named J.D. in that Ventura motel the night of the Northridge quake?

She let her cigarette fall to her feet and stepped on it with her hiking shoe.

—When you described your brother I knew it was him. Nothing happened. I didn't sleep with him.

-72-

—It's none of my business what you did with him..and I don't want to ever judge you..but I've got to call my sister and find out if she knows any other reason why we're connected to my brother and if it's going to make my life better.

—I think you're supposed to write about this in your next book..as it happens. Don't you see, Dwayne? This is some great gift you've been given. I'm going to write about it..but I don't have the readers you have. It's all meant to help your writing. Lighten up and have fun with it. It's a small world..and a short life.

I took another cigarette from her pocket and lit one for her, too, while I thought about what she said.

—You're right. I want to go write about it.

—While you write..I'll read 'The Paper Man'.

That night while Vee had been reading in the bedroom on my bed under a reading light, I wrote up a storm at Traveller's booth. Right from the start she liked the story and she could see that it would make a terrific movie. Josie was the female lead, the young girl the Paper Man pursued, loved and possessed until she left him alone in his territory again. That's where we were now, closing in on the Paper Man's territory from the north.

I was writing about it now how I never approached this area from the north. A hundred times before I had traveled west across South Dakota to the Paper Man's sacred territory.

Earlier I had called Karen and told her I was planning on getting a cabin with Vee in the Black Hills. Karen told me that according to the chart that Vee would be healthy for me, and, in fact, healthy for both of us according to our integrated charts. She told me that together we radiate gold, the color of health, for two hundred miles in any direction. Outside Traveller on my cell phone, pacing fifty yards away, I told Karen about Culver City. She said that Vee was a touchstone for our brother John. I asked her sarcastically if that means a good lay. She told me that maybe that's part of it, but it's all good, and I should have a good time with her from where she sits. I sighed, knowing my sister would gladly trade places from her wheelchair. She said she was getting checks from my libraries at a good clip and that she would e-mail some orders that came in. She said since I told her I would sell around Rapid City that she'd get me some signings lined up. I agreed, since I planned on being in the Black Hills area for a week or two. I told her to keep the signings to a 50-mile radius from Custer. And then I told her how beautiful Vee is. My sister said:

—Yeah..and she's only fifteen years younger than you, bro. think you're beginning to mature.

—Hey! If Vee was fifty I'd be with her. The timing was so perfect, Karen, with her just getting a divorce when I met her. And she had time to go with me on this run because she has to wait a month for her divorce settlement. Your chart really hit the mark for romance. But what about the purple..the mystery?

—Well, enjoy good health in your old territory, Paper Man, and stay alert for the mystery when you take her home. Just make sure her ex isn't waiting for you.

She watched him talking to Karen from Traveller's bedroom window with one hand book marking her place in 'The Paper Man'. Something bothered her about the story. Not halfway into his novel and he had captured the essence of Vee's life in his character Josie. She could see herself playing Josie as if the part had been written for her. She wanted to run out to him and tell him how she was born to play Josie in the film and that may be the reason they came together.

When she saw him light a stick from her pack she exited Traveller. That's when she heard him tell his sister that he loved her; then, he clicked off his phone and handed her the pack of smokes.

—Karen says hi.
Vee smiled, adding:

—That's sweet. Did she say anything about my chart?

—She said that we're in a healthy space.
They laughed when he raised his cigarette to his lips; she put the pack in her pocket without getting one to smoke.

—I'm in a space of vacillating between quitting and

cheating.

He stepped on his butt:

    —Me, too.

    It was after dark when she made us dinner: microwaved chicken with rice and broccoli and a salad with iced tea; she wanted to make our first meal in Traveller a salubrious one in this territory of gold. At the booth we discussed plans:

    —I'd like to get a cabin near Custer, I said.

    —Like Josie and Harvey? she smiled.

    —I know the same cabin they stayed in.

    —Did you write the script of 'The Paper Man'?

    —Yeah, but it's an earlier version before the novel.

    —So you wouldn't submit it to agents and producers?

    —No.

    —You going to write another script for it? Hollywood's always looking for a good dramatic comedy.

    —I live well off my books. If someone wants to write the script adapted from the book..so be it. Not me.

    —Can I write it?

I looked up from my plastic compartment tray on my plate and she added that she could finish it in two weeks if she focused on it.

    —Why would you want to write someone else's story?

    —I like it.

    —Have you written any before?

    —No, but I've worked with enough scripts in acting class to do it..with your help. I know I could, Dwayne.

    —What would you want if someone bought the rights from me?

    —I don't know. We can work that out. I think it would be fun.

    —If that's what you call fun..have fun.

    —Thank you. The spine of the story is there. I already have an idea for the beginning scene.

She got up and came over and gave me a big kiss on my mouth, staying with the kiss as she did in Culver City in my hotel room.

Afterwards I whispered:

—Is my breath as bad as yours?

She laughed with me until she thought more on it:

—You are talking about my cigarette breath?

—Our breath, I smiled, then kissed her quick.

Then she kissed my chin and told me she wanted to finish my book and get started on the script.

From my recliner I watched a movie on the screen above Traveller's windshield. The reception was fizzy, but the Rapid City station was the only one I could get in this isolated part of the Midwest.

Around midnight, I ditched outside for a smoke, but thought of the gold and decided not to; instead, I walked up and down the long entrance road waiting for Vee to finish the story. It wasn't long before I saw Traveller's bathroom light come on and heard her taking a shower. I was very anxious for her feedback.

I was seated at the booth under the light when she came out of the bathroom smiling with a brown bath towel covering her breasts to the top of her thighs.

—I finished it. Do you have the music?

While she put on beige shorts with a white belly T-shirt I played the Boz Scaggs song 'Danger There's a Breakdown Dead Ahead'. I told her this is the race song above the music coming from only the bedroom speakers. She said:

—And with Huck in Pine Ridge?

—Yeah.

It was so beautiful to me to see her listening so intently to the music. She was the only person who I could see visualizing my scenes with the music. Seven times she had me play the song while she scribbled notes at the booth and talked to me:

—The lead boy in the van presses the start button for the song to begin with two large stereo speakers on top of the van's roof. Then, when the song begins, Huck's ears perk up behind his muzzle in his starting chute. The electric bunny starts to move toward the chute area. Right..here..the chutes open and the dogs bolt out. The race is choreographed with shots back and forth of

Harvey and Josie urging Huck on as Huck makes his way from behind the pack. Yes! Yes! I can see it! Dwayne, it's the perfect song for Huck's race and at Pine Ridge!

—Remember to keep it all in present tense, I said.

—Yes, I remember that scripts are written in present tense. Even flashbacks?

—Yes. I'll get you a script to follow format. Ya know that Hollywood doesn't really believe good movies have many flashbacks.

—This one has to have them.

—I agree. 'Forrest Gump' was loaded with flashbacks.

—That whole movie was a flashback, she laughed. With Forrest on a bench waiting for a bus..all the way to the end.

—I sat on that same bench in Charleston.

—In South Carolina?

—Yeah, I answered while digging in a box until I found my script for "The Paper Man".

When I handed it to her I reminded her that it's different from my book and I told her to read the beginning while I turned off the music. Then I sat down with her and this is what we read together:

FADE IN:

EXT. PAPER MAN VAN - NIGHT

On an isolated country road in rural South Dakota, Steve Winwood's song 'Talking Back to the Night' plays from a parked white van that's rocking from sexual activity inside the van. On the side of the van is vehicle lettering: THE PAPER MAN

Paper & Janitorial Supplies
FREE DELIVERY

EXT. RAILROAD TRACKS

200 yards away from van a slim Labrador/shepherd dog HUCK sniffs ground between tracks when sees: (Huck's POV)

EXT. TRAIN HEADLIGHT APPROACHING &

EXT. PAPER MAN VAN

The van moves slowly in reverse toward tracks.

EXT. RAILROAD TRACKS

HUCK barks at van to warn couple in van.

INT. PAPER MAN VAN
HARVEY & JOSIE, married, are oblivious to van moving while passionate sex in sleeping bag with loud music.
EXT. RAILROAD TRACKS
Huck runs for van as fast-moving freight train closes in on tracks where van is slowly headed.
INT. PAPER MAN VAN
Above the music they reach climax as train nears and Huck squeals from pain when van stops short of tracks.
EXT. PAPER MAN VAN
As the train speeds by just missing the back of the stopped van we see Huck blocking back tire with his body. (CUT TO)
INT. VETERINARIAN EXAM ROOM - LATER
Harvey, 40-year-old toilet paper salesman, and Josie, 30-year-old, attractive with Native American bloodline, watch anxiously as a Custer Vet. examines Huck on his exam table.

CUSTER VET
Looks like some bruised ribs.
No signs of internal bleeding.
I should take some x-rays.

JOSIE
Will he be okay?

CUSTER VET
Should be as good as new in
a couple weeks.

HARVEY
He's gotta race in two weeks, Doc.

CUSTER VET
He should be fine. Huck's a smart
dog. I can't figure out how he got
pinned under your van.

Josie and Harvey are ashamed of themselves.

HARVEY

It's my fault, Doc. He was sleeping under the van..and I left the
transmission in neutral. It happened so fast..

JOSIE

Harvey, don't be so hard on
yourself. You forgot.

Huck looks at Harvey & Josie with sad eyes. They bow their heads
in shame.

I stopped Vee from reading on. I asked her if she liked the
beginning.

—Yes, I really do. It has suspense and humor. It really held
my interest. I wouldn't change it at all. It's better than my idea. I
want to finish reading the script.

I got two beers out of the fridge and opened them. My toast:

—To the Hills.

She picked up on those same words she read in 'The Paper Man'.

—One bed, she smiled.

—I hope so.

We laughed.

We made love in Traveller's bedroom 'til three in the
morning. There was no music or talk about happily ever after.
Only sleep. Deep sleep. The kind of sleep that once you
awaken–the world has changed and anything's possible. I knew this
the moment my consciousness told me I was alive for another day.
Truly alive.

I felt it in my legs, the second place on a man's body when
he knows he's been with a special woman who he wants to be with
again and again. The usual stiffness in my legs had moved north,

just like when I was in my roaring 20s.

She was up early. A good sign for her. For several months she had dreaded the morning and where it was leading.

Intoxicating morning smells and sounds were all over Traveller's interior: fried potatoes and onions sizzling in olive oil; the sound of her voice when she called out "How do you want your eggs?"; and the strong aroma of fresh-brewed freeze-dried coffee stored in a Tupperware sandwich-sized container that her mother gave her as a wedding gift.

After brushing my teeth and washing my face in the bathroom sink, I sat at the booth in my black boxers and a clean/white V-neck T-shirt. The blinds were twisted open to the gray sky covering the Badlands. On the middle of the table a gold plastic water glass held a mixed bunch of gray lavender caspia and some solid aster that was yellow/green. Vee had picked them early this morning after writing a bit on the script when she went outside to have a smoke. At the time, neither of us knew the names of the flowers in the glass. After I brought them to my nose I breathed deeply and commented on the beauty of their combined colors. Then, I placed the makeshift vase closer to the window where these laser shards of morning light splashed over them, giving them this brilliant acrylic illumination as if lit by bright gallery lights. We watched it together and held the moment without speaking.

I wanted to write about this feeling of new love I hadn't felt since my paper man days. Frightful/joy was there, even stronger now after we'd made love for the first time. As we ate our breakfast I asked her:

—I feel this frightful/joy when I'm around you. Do you feel it, too?

—That's an interesting description. Yes..it's stronger now. What do you think it is?

—I think it's the fear of loss..abandonment. When someone or something good happens..it's that wanting to hold on..

—To not let go when it changes, she added.

—Exactly.

We continued eating without speaking, each of us glancing

at the other when the other wasn't looking. I could feel this desire in me to hold onto her now, to say or do something new that kept her interested in me. After she refilled my coffee mug with the inscription 'Success Is Loving What You Do' I said to her:

—One of the reasons I follow my sister's chart and believe in it is because I believe that most people are not where they are supposed to be.

—Literally or consciously?

—Both. Not that I'm more conscious than most people..but I do see more unhappiness than joy in this world. It's mostly in the eyes and face..around the mouth..where I see this in people I meet and don't know.

—Most people are a bit guarded and shut down around strangers..don't you think?

—Sure..and Karen's chart has shown me I can experience a better life. Ninety-nine percent of the time off the chart I feel as if I'm only existing. Her chart brought me to Minot..to you. That's where I was to hopefully find this left-handed town that would spark my writing. And love. For a thousand miles I imagined I would meet this perfect woman in this left-handed town in North Dakota. We would swim naked in the wind-whipped waves of Devils Lake and make love in secret places in this town that held this secret about how the town founders knew that left-handed people live together in harmony because of the way the human brain is wired. But it was the place..the location of this town that made every thing and person work so well together.

When I took a bite of my eggs and potatoes she said:

—Uh huh..like when your body feels right..in a certain place..but then it goes away.

I nodded yes while chewing and taking a drink of coffee. She went on to say that she felt that way in Culver City when we were both there. I agreed and told her that I didn't feel this same frightful/joy like I do now. After ruminating, she agreed and added:

—This frightful/joy is like the perfect fear. It's like I want it to go away..but something about it feels so good.

—I felt it the strongest when I first met you in the

café..when I played the jukebox.

—And you danced with your shoulders, she laughed.
I dipped my shoulders to demonstrate.

—I really thought you were so sexy, she confessed.

—It was the same song one of my characters sang in 'Shy Ann'. That's when I knew you were the mystery girl I was supposed to find in North Dakota. But I still don't get how easy it was to find you. I mean..I really thought I'd have to scour half the state and somehow find you after many miles and weeks of searching for that left-handed town.

—And there I was, she beamed.

—There you were.

After breakfast we showered together..to save water. We made love before going for a walk. We went east this time, into the sun, until we reached a dry gulch that was made of this brittle red clay that gave way under our feet as if walking on eggshells.

Vee talked about the five pages she wrote on 'The Paper Man' script before I got up. She said she stayed with my version for the most part. She talked about how she wanted to get a cabin in the Black Hills just as Harvey and Josie did in the story, in order to get a feel for their romantic stay there before the breakdown dead ahead. I said I wanted to work Rapid City, sell some books for a couple hours and have some signings in Rapid, Custer and Lead.

—What about Pine Ridge? she asked.

—Too poor. They can't buy any books.

—Can we go there? It would really help me with the script. Please, Harvey.

I Smell Smoke

I hit Rapid City like gang busters while my new/beautiful girlfriend worked on the script in Traveller. Often, I sold two or three books to multiple readers in one business. Vee was responsible for that. As I sit here alone, writing at a table in the Rapid City library, waiting for the director to return to the library from lunch–I'm happier than I believe I've ever been. There's such a big difference when someone special is in my life who makes me yearn to return to her, to see her again, again, and again.

Vicky Derryberry from L.A. is by far the most captivating woman I've ever met. Maybe I have not gotten to know enough truly incredible women in my life to make such a statement, but I've sure as hell seen enough women to know that she's at the top of my 'visions of beauty' list.

Any minute I know I will be on my way to see her. I know now what that walk will be like. I will notice a thousand things around me that I normally would not if I were alone. And I will let them all go, because my mind often returns to her. It returns to her hazel eyes that changed from a thousand uncertainties to genuine fondness and affection. Forget about love and trust. Those things will come later if we want them for ourselves. I do not trust her or love her yet. Trust is not always a part of loving someone. I've loved and yet not trusted the same person. For now, I'm enjoying this summer of '02 without expectations. Life is good.

On my walk to Traveller it was just as I wrote about. The colors of summer in Rapid City were not as drab as the last summer I was here. And I popped in and out of select businesses and made quick sales with Henry riding my hip just like Floyd/Harvey in 'The Paper Man'. Yes, Vee had sparked me to the point I wanted to be: total aliveness.

During my three hours of selling time today I had made

enough money to rent a cabin in the Black Hills for a week. Love is money that way. In fact, I called Karen and told her not to schedule any signings in this area yet.

'Nights with Vee', I kept repeating to myself, and 'God, I'm lucky'.

As I was walking by the Rapid City Federal Building, it reminded me of a scene I wanted Vee to add to the script. First I had to discuss it with her. I had sold all 15 books that I had packed in Henry earlier with only three blocks to go until I would reach the Wal-Mart parking lot where Traveller was parked. A fear about Traveller being stolen crossed my mind because I couldn't see my home from this distance. I walked faster.

When I entered Traveller from the side door Vee was writing up a storm and unable to talk until she finished writing the scene she was on. So, I showered though anxious to talk to her about the script before heading for the 'hills'.

After I showered I laid back spread-eagle on my bed with nothing on except for a towel that covered my middle. When I opened my eyes Vee was standing there at the side of the bed looking down at me with her sexy almond-shaped green eyes and smiling without showing her teeth.

—You don't show your teeth when you smile. I just noticed that.

—I don't like my teeth. They're too small for my mouth.

—You mean your mouth's too big? I laughed.
She pulled off my towel and snapped me with it, accidentally hitting one of my gonads, causing me to jump three inches off the bed and yell 'OW!'. She sat next to me laughing while I examined my sore thing.

On the way to Custer Vee talked about the script. I told her about this scene that I thought gave the ending more humor. Parked on the Mt. Rushmore parking lot in Keystone I found an older version of the script. I was really impressed that she read it right away without wanting to see Mt. Rushmore. This is what she read:

EXT. SMALL TOWN MAIN STREET - DAY
Summertime. Harvey is selling to businesses door to door.
INT. PARKED PAPER MAN VAN
Josie is napping on the front passenger seat with her shapely bare
legs extended to dash.
INT. REDNECKS' PICKUP
Two REDNECKS parked nearby stare at Josie's legs.

REDNECK #1
Five bucks a yam?

REDNECK #2
Yer on.

EXT. PARKED PAPER MAN VAN
Josie smiles with her eyes closed when she thinks Harvey is
touching her legs sensually. She opens her eyes and bolts up upon
seeing Redneck #1 grinning at her. She rolls up her window, locks
door as rednecks press faces to glass laughing, then walk away.
INT. PARKED PAPER MAN VAN
Josie panics when sees keys are not in ignition. In glove box
looking for spare she finds her wedding band. She looks back at
ominous case of TP marked for 'Dennis'.
INT. SMALL TOWN BAR
Harvey enters bar with sales case and stands at end of bar near
same two rednecks having a beer. Bartender greets Harvey.

BARTENDER
Whatcha got?

Harvey hands bartender a product card.

HARVEY
A good buy on some
toilet paper.

The rednecks laugh obnoxiously.

BARTENDER
Is it soft?

More laughter.

HARVEY
You don't want soft in a
bar..unless you take some
home with ya.

REDNECK #1
How 'bout corncobs, Paper Man?
Ya can't poke yer fingers through corncobs!

Laughter from Rednecks and locals.

HARVEY
On second thought..looks like ya could use 2-ply..
to cover the big assholes that come in here.

Rednecks do not laugh with locals and bartender.

EXT. PARKED PAPER MAN VAN
Josie rolls down window when Harvey approaches and he opens
van's side door and removes 2-wheeler from cargo bed.

JOSIE
Can we get out of this town?

HARVEY
(Loads TP)
After this delivery.

Josie sees trouble approaching as both rednecks appear.

REDNECK #1
We'd like to have a case of that TP, Paper Man.

HARVEY
Sorry, I'm sold out.

Redneck #1 sees the case of TP marked for 'Dennis'.

REDNECK #1
There's a case right there!

HARVEY
It's sold.

REDNECK #1
We'll just take it off yer hands.

As Redneck #2 moves Harvey out of the way, Redneck #1 starts to climb into van but stops upon hearing a GROWL behind him. All turn and see Huck with sales collar and red hanky around his neck bearing teeth at rednecks.

HARVEY
Did ya know that you can
get aids if a gay dog bites ya?

The rednecks look at each other scared and confused and then back away from the van. Huck jumps into cargo area as rednecks retreat to Josie's relief.

We sat at one of the many tables in the cafeteria looking out at Mt. Rushmore while having coffee and apple pie. We discussed the script and debated whether to put it in the script she was working on. Vee said:
—I liked the scene with the rednecks. Huck comes to the rescue again and it adds suspense and humor.

—They show up that night..

—The rednecks? Vee asks and writes down notes.

—Yeah, with a gun. They threaten to rape Josie and take the race money..and when they try to take the TP in the van...

—Which threatens the mission in Pine Ridge.

—Right. Anyway, Huck comes to the rescue again, bites one of the rednecks on his ass and Harvey has Huck kiss the other redneck on his mouth.

—They think they have aids, Vee laughed.

—Yes, and there's a funny scene at the Rapid City Federal Building where the rednecks are waiting in the crowd to club Harvey with a tire iron after Harvey's trial. But Josie pushes the rednecks into FBI agents who are struck by the rednecks..so they're arrested right away.

—That's good! And since the rednecks are not critical to the storyline..it adds curiosity and humor..plus Josie's seen as a protagonist early on.

—Right..but that's what bothers me. I see the beginning of the film with all these small town locals running to a TV set to see Harvey's verdict.

As Vee writes feverishly to keep up, I went on:

—While Harvey's in the conference room with his attorney before the verdict..his attorney can't get Harvey to rat on Josie.

—He still loves her.

—Right. So Harvey goes into the restroom alone..finds the planted music/cassette player with a pinjoint.

Vee continued excitedly:

—Yes! That's when 'Talking Back to the Night' comes on during the rocking van scene with the train and Huck's rescue to stop the van from hitting the train.

—But where next?

—To the courtroom and his guilty verdict and sentence..and then to the crowd outside where Josie pushes the rednecks into the FBI agents before Harvey is driven off to jail.

—Where next? I asked.

—That's where Harvey flashes back while handcuffed in the

police car.

　　—To where?

　　—To the race!

　　—No..too early. Remember..Huck's recovering from his trip to the vet after the near train accident.

　　—Oh, that's right.

Just then, my eyes widened from a sudden dawning.

　　—What? she asked, looking hard at me.

　　—They're in the Black Hills..here..in the cabin. Huck's recovering there.

　　—Good! Let's go get a cabin!

As we exited the cafeteria we stopped and took a quick look together at Mt. Rushmore before leaving in a hurry hand in hand.

　　As Traveller cruised slowly among the beautiful Black Hills I played the wedding song in 'The Paper Man' 'Isn't It Time' by Boz Scaggs while Vee wrote from the passenger seat. Behind the wheel I imagined what it will be like in the cabin with Vee:

　　I saw us making love by candlelight in the old cabin on an antique bed. As the music played: I could see us walking in the hills holding hands. I see us eating healthy candlelit meals at our rustic cabin table. Again I see us making love, this time in front of the burning fireplace.

　　I stopped at two realtors and none of them had the cabin I wanted or any rentals available by the day or for a week. Since businesses were closing for the day I parked in the Custer library parking lot for the night, and would look for a cabin tomorrow.

　　For an hour we walked along the Custer main drag that was a highway that stretched for five miles from one end of town to the other. We talked about the script until I told Vee that I was amazed how she could be so interested in it. She told me that it's a great project and that it could be sold in L.A. with no problem at all. I responded:

　　—Ya know..I'm so jaded from that specious L.A. scene and submitting my scripts that never get read. That's why I like sellin' my books. I at least get readers.

—I hear what you say. I just know I could get your script read in L.A., Dwayne. I see a bidding war for 'The Paper Man' very fast.

I looked at her as if she was kidding, and finally said:

—Are you kidding?

—No, I'm not kidding, Dwayne. I'm dead serious.

—I smell smoke.

She laughed.

About when we turned back and headed for Traveller she squeezed my hand and looked at me while we walked, explaining how when she was a young girl in Culver City she would sneak into Sony Studios just to see if she could. A hundred times she said she'd gotten past the security guards, and that each time was a different time of day. She told me how she would roam the massive studio lot and think of ways she would become a star, until one day she decided to write her way into stardom.

—Writer/in, I called it.

I stopped her from walking by taking her notebook and the pen that was clipped to it. I printed Writer/In like this, explaining how the slash between Writer and In is a door that I have been trying to knock down for so long. Just then: I saw this thing that was so beautiful. I saw the girl Vicky Derryberry embrace those two words I had printed, pressing the notebook to her chest. She stammered her first words, telling me she thought that this could be their left-handed town, that we were lefties who came together to become this Writer/In in a right-handed world of politics, waiting, and dying dreams.

I pulled her to me at her shoulders with her hands yet holding her notebook between them. We started to cry; she started it for me when I felt her holding on so tight to her dream with those slender arms of hers that had kept holding onto those girlhood days in Culver City for all these years. Thin arms that had delivered and balanced and cleared ten thousand plates of food and dirty dishes. And it was the same dream my brother and I once had for making my stories into independent videos.

When I leaned back to look at her I could see that those

big/bright hazel eyes were falling in love with me. Perhaps I could see her this way because I felt that she could really see me. I thought I noticed it in her smile when she returned with my order the first time I met her. Her lips were pursed up and pooched out as if the sight of me was tickling her.

I kissed her until I could feel myself falling with her while trembling against her small breasts on this late, gray afternoon in Custer. Falling in love with this beautiful waitress who believed in my work more than anyone I'd ever met. Was this why I was falling? Was it because she was in love with writing my trivial imagined story that nobody else on earth had read with the same ardor?

She would tell him one day that this was the second time she fell in love. For she still believed in love at first sight; when she saw him shoulder dancing to the same song she played once a week, to remind her that she was happy to be 'the game'-as long as she was captured by a hunter who loved her and empowered all her dreams. He would understand her failed marriage and why she left town with him, a stranger who she also found, a man who could make her move closer to her potential. For she saw herself as Josie in every way and then some. Yes, she wanted more than anything to play Josie and to tell him so before he felt used by some slick chick from LA. But the timing wasn't right. Perhaps he will see it himself before I tell him, she thought. Or, perhaps he already does.

Just then: a tall/lean German pointer with his shaggy coat of black and gray/white walked lazily by us. Then he stopped and lowered his magnificent brown head with these bushy-brown eyebrows that were inches long, above sad/brown eyes as big as liquid marbles.

We separated and giggled at the dog's sorry countenance and contrite walk. At the same instant: I thought it; she said it:

—Huck has to be found.

We continued walking. She told me that we have to find Huck, and that he's the key to selling the script. I agreed, yet had no clue about just how Huck, the Paper Man's sales-collared dog and best friend, would sell my script. I stated that we'd have to be in L.A.

She said nothing, wanting it to be his idea, and she was not really sure that her idea was good for him. Dwayne said:

—We can finish the library book signing 'round here..and see where this all goes.

—I could have the script written and printed if I stay on it. My printer's broken, but I can get it printed on three-hole paper in Rapid City or Custer if we're in this area.

When we reached the Custer library where Traveller was parked I wanted Vee to go inside the library with me. I took her hand in mine and lead her up to the reference desk in the middle of the air conditioned building.

—Are you the head librarian?

—Yes.

—I am D. H. Dayne. My sister might've contacted you about having a book signing here this week.

—Oh, yes, she smiled back after shaking hands.

—Can you tell me how my books circulate here? I'd love to know.

The librarian went to her computer screen and found my books on her database catalog records:

—'Ledges'..ten times..'Paper Man' and 'Missouri Madness' fifteen checkouts each.

—That's not too bad. I'll bring you a copy of 'Shy Ann' with invoice at the signing.

—That'll be fine, Mr. Dayne.

—Oh, I can sell my books, right?

—Yes, of course. We're just happy to have authors visit us.

—Thanks. See ya soon.

We left the library still holding hands. Vee was thinking out loud:

—Most of the dogs trained for film are in Simi Valley.

—Isn't that where a lot of cops retire?

—Yeah, along with Rin Tin Tin and Lassie.

I told her that after the signings 'round here we could go to

Simi Valley because Huck's the key to the story getting sold.

She knew she was playing it down when she told Dwayne that it all sounds like a great idea and opportunity. In fact, it was during her last session with Butch in her hotel room that he told her it was okay with him if she wasn't in Minot for their divorce settlement day; and that he would make it easy for her. All because Butch knew that she could nail him bad on the base if they tested him for pot use; he'd be booted out of the service without benefits.

She didn't think that Dwayne needed to know that now; and, she knows he's been thinking about writing a scene he wanted to put in his next title.

—Why don't you write that scene about that motel clerk while I take a quick shower. I'll read what you write. Deadlines make things get done.

I was scrawling on paper from Blacky's folder after Vee had showered and had been working on the script at the front passenger seat. I was writing about when I was a paper salesman, in the throes of getting thirty sales per day from at least a hundred calls in my South Dakota territory:

Beresford was always a tough town to sell in. Off Highway 29 that ran north and south, Beresford was between Sioux City and Sioux Falls. Just a quarter-mile from the Beresford exit was an isolated motel, privately owned. When I entered the registration area I had no idea that I would meet a man, a stranger who would affect my life a thousand times. He was a thin man of medium height with black hair slicked back permanently from taking orders from his dominating wife. From the unbearable sound of his wife's voice demanding that her husband get out to the desk I knew he was as henpecked as no other grown man I'd ever seen in my life.

Before he came out from behind the drab smoke-stained curtain that divided the front desk from their dark cubbyhole apartment, I could smell fried food mixed with stale cigarette smoke coming from their space. When this man came out I knew I'd seen the most whipped dog of a man I'd every lay eyes on. Besides his palsy, his weakest feature was his passive/faltering voice that kept repeating "No..don't need a thing today." And then he'd let out this gasp of air as if his words had just been painfully squeezed from his bowels.

Yes, he was the wimp I feared to become one day, if I ever found myself in a life unlived. That motel clerk would be the one person that would snap me out of a cowardly spell when I felt weak and lonely; or when I was settling for a girl who wasn't good for me; and all those times when I doubted my future to prosper and live out my dreams. It was that milk toast motel clerk in Beresford who pulled me out of it, every single time.

Writing about him now: validates my experience as a paper man. I have never wondered what happened to him, yet I have wondered a thousand times if he could happen to me.

Being a single man in my roaring 20s, I have been amazed at least a hundred times by the raw physical beauty of Midwest women. In Iowa, Nebraska, Minnesota, and South Dakota, in obscure rural businesses in these little towns, I have been totally flabbergasted by every beautiful woman I'd see, like one particular small town local, was waiting in her chiropractor's office, wearing such nice/clean clothes and poised good posture; it was rather obvious that her inner beauty in the gentle quietness of her nature for simple things that told me to never settle for the henpecked life of that motel clerk.

I'm Late

After writing about the motel clerk, I showered while Vee was working now on the script on the bed on her belly. She was really moving along at a good clip, using my novel as a guide. When I came into the bedroom to dry off she told me that the whole film is a flashback except for the beginning and the ending.

—I know. I couldn't get around that.

—Only a young director would do it, she said.

—Maybe.

—I can see Jim Carrey playing the Paper Man, she said.

—You really think you could sell the script that fast?

She nodded yes.

—Why don't we head out to L.A. then? I said.

I saw her reaction change from surprise to open, then I asked her if that would be too far from Minot for her settlement.

—I can handle that. Butch won't be a problem. And I have all my stuff with me. It's all good, Dwayne.

—Will you have the script finished?

—Yes! It's going so smoothly. I follow the book mostly.

—I still wanna get a cabin here.

—Me, too.

She met my kiss when I bent down to her. I said:

—I don't know if you're the best thing that's ever happened to me..or if I'm being led straight into hell.

She laughed on my neck, and said:

—Devil or angel.

—Maybe a little of each, I laughed.

I sat down on the bed beside her and gazed into those hazel eyes. I could see that she was happy the way things were going since we got together in Minot. I said:

—Look, we don't have to have a cabin. What do you say that tomorrow we find a place 'round here to park Traveller..okay?

—Sounds good to me. I like your home. Dwayne..I have to
tell you something.
I laid back, thinking she was going to talk about the script.
—I'm late, she said.
I could feel myself blinking several times as I listened:
—My period. I was supposed to have it about two weeks
ago.
—Have you been late before?
—Yeah..but I'm usually right on schedule.
—Your divorce..all that stress..that could be why.
—Yeah..I hope so.
—When will you know for sure?
—I s'pose I could get one of those pregnancy test kits at a
drugstore.
—Wouldn't you rather know and not have to worry about
it?
—No, I don't want to know if I am..while workin' on your
script. It would distract me too much.
—I understand. You'll probably have it soon, I smiled and
hoped.
—Oh! I wanted to ask you if we could stop in my
hometown in Kansas. My grandpa lives there. I moved away from
there when I was three.
—What's the name of the town?
—Minneapolis.
—In Kansas?
—Uh huh.
—Where is it?
—I know it's not far from Nebraska.
—I don't see a problem.
—Good. I haven't seen my grandpa since I was twelve. I
exhaled deeply, brushing back her short blonde/auburn hair so thick
and full between my fingers. She watched me looking at her hair
and I said:
—Hair has always been the number one feature I see on a
woman. I want you to talk to me about your grandpa. Your life in

Kansas. I want to know it all. I get so bored with my own selfish patterns. I need to hear things from you that pull me out of it. I need to listen and really imagine your experiences.

She hugged me and kissed my lips, keeping close to my mouth when she said:

—If you get me started..I'll never shut up.

At that moment I was certain that I saw love in her eyes, or could it be the thrill of returning to her roots in Kansas. She kept her face close to me while laughing that goofy laugh she thought so unattractive.

—I love your laugh. But you keep it from coming out. You seem to shut it down.

She nodded in agreement, smiling, kissing my nose, listening:

—Nothing is more attractive to me or inspires more confidence than to hear your laugh. Do it more. I love it.

—I'll work on it, she smiled.

I moved up the signing to the next evening in Custer. Only four people showed besides Vee. Two of the four had read my books. I sold only two copies plus the library's one, not to mention one that Vee bought to break the ice. It was when I addressed the small audience from a table:

—Can you hear me out there?

That's when Vee really let out her goofy laugh. Later she told me about how it felt good to laugh so loud. At least ten times I heard her laugh in the room of the old library.

After the signing, on our short walk to Traveller, Vee jumped into my arms and straddled my waist, kissing me several times while we laughed at the wonderful sound of her awakened true laugh.

Inside Traveller, she wanted to play. This morning she found out in the drugstore's restroom that she wasn't pregnant.

She tore off her Black Hills T-shirt she bought there with her kit and ran for the bedroom. After closing all the curtains I played the Boz Scaggs song 'Heart of Mine' and headed for the bedroom. As the song played, she was already under the covers laughing louder than she ever had with a lover or friend.

Three nights in a row we laughed all the way through the poor showing at each library in Rapid, Lead and Hot Springs. After I sold four books in Hot Springs we headed south into Nebraska at night. Vee worked on the script at Traveller's booth under a lone light shining on her word processor as she went from an old script to novel to new text.

I could see her lovely head craned down while biting down on a pencil. Every once in a while she would call out to me or come up behind me and ask me if this or that idea worked; or, if a character's dialog sounded good to me. I could hardly believe that such an attractive woman was interested in my work. In fact, I couldn't remember even anyone interested in my work.

I felt like driving all night. Vee went to bed around two in the morning after spending a half-hour on the passenger seat going over what she'd written.

Around seven that morning, Vee woke up alone in the dark bedroom. She didn't hear Dwayne up front or remember him coming to bed at all during the night.

—Dwayne? she called out to the front of Traveller.

She got out of bed and twisted open a bedroom shade, surprised to see that she was in her girlhood hometown. The one remarkable thing that Minneapolis, Kansas ever had was there a hundred feet away in a field. She put on her jean cut-offs and a belly T-shirt before running barefoot toward a freakish natural wonder that was bigger than life to her some three decades ago.

Dwayne was leaning against one of the seven massive brindle-colored balls of solid rock that Kansas prairie winds over thousands of years had whipped and wound into 12-foot-tall boulders as big as a one-stall garage.

—Now these are some cool rocks, he said.

She kissed me on my cheek and I held her in front of me with her back to me and talked softly in her ear:

—I could see the trees of the town's park after crossing the little bridge by the river. The sun was just coming up when I saw these..rocks. My eyes were tired..and I thought..well..I didn't know what I was seeing. I wanted you to wake up so we could see this together.

—I can remember when I was about three..and we had a picnic here. These boulders were my first impression of just how big the world is. Other than my grandpa's house..this place stands out as being home again.

—Do you consider L.A. or here your home?

—Both.

I could hear her short fingernails, worn down from waitress work, scratching ever so lightly over the smooth purplish brown surface of the massive boulder before she said:

—Geologists say these were formed from one grain of sand.

—I read about them over there, I pointed.

I kissed her hair at the back of her head and lifted her hair to kiss her neck. It tickled her.

—I need a walk. Show me your town.

She turned around and faced my tired eyes, keeping her rested eyes on mine. I picked a speck of sleep from her left eye, smiling at the notion that the ten tons of rock against my back was once this small.

—I want to get my shoes and brush my teeth, she said.

—I'll wait here.

I watched her perfect shape move away and disappear behind one of these smooth giants. During the night behind the wheel somewhere in southern Nebraska, I could see Vee playing my character Josie on the big screen. And I realized that she could be interested in my script just to get a shot at playing Josie. Time and again I'd see her play the music from the script, and I thought I saw her imagining herself playing Josie. I marveled at how perfect she would be for the part, and how she was even more suited to play Josie than anyone else I could imagine.

I yawned, arching my back while raising my arms overhead to stretch for the new Kansas sky that was turning to a milky baby blue as a new morning dawned. Somehow, I knew I had to put it out there that I was open to her playing my Josephine. For I knew if chicanery was at all any part of her reasons for being with me-I would have to lose her, because I could never stand to be lied to, especially by a woman I was willing to love. Yet this one glaring physical fact remained: Vee was beautiful/smart and has the ability to possibly make me a Writer/In, leading me to produce my own films without any Hollywood influence. So, I knew I had to let her lead the way into L.A. and give up 'The Paper Man' to make her dream come true even though I thought 'the business' a lousy one to say the least.

This root cause of frightful/joy yet remained in my belly, living like the parasite it was. For the first time, I could put it on my tongue and say it out loud. Against these monolithic boulders that I would find nowhere else on earth if I searched for a thousand years, as I heard the girl of my ten thousand dreams coming, her face fresh from the splash of Traveller's water, my words came out and hit those hazel eyes as if she'd discovered something new:

—What good will we do after 'The Paper Man' is out?

She continued walking toward him, knowing for the first time that the ending of 'The Paper Man' was where they were now. Together on this incredible journey, she had to reveal her true self now or continue being estranged from real love. When she took his left hand from his side into her right hand and leaned back against the magic rock made by billions of invisible winds-the spinning began, clockwise this time, forward and forward, swirling in a green mist of prosperity, to a moment they willed together like an inchoate scream-lost forever between their fingers, their squeeze, and invisible winds.

For Lefties Only

She had never looked or felt better in her 33 years. Vee is her professional name now, she had told the studio executive's secretary, and:

—Please tell Mr. Friedman I have but fifteen minutes before I have to leave for my next appointment.

Vee sat in the waiting area alone, expecting to be seen right on time vs. the usual stall by another Jewish Hollywood big shot. Just then:

—Vee..Mr. Friedman will see you now.

To her feet, brushing away any possible wrinkles on her black slacks, she resented those words "Mr. Friedman will see you now." He's lucky I'm here to be seen, she thought as she followed the secretary into Mr. Friedman's expansive office. She entered the office wearing the $200 pearl-colored blouse Dwayne bought her in Beverly Hills yesterday.

Vee's confident beauty forced the tanned middle-aged executive to stand and swipe his reading glasses from the middle of his Jewish snoz. Friedman couldn't remember the last time he'd done that. Her smile was flat and as uninviting as it ever was; she took over their meeting from the start by extending her left hand to handshake with the confused executive, explaining:

—I only shake with my left hand. I'm from a town where everyone is left handed. The right hand is sinister to us. Friedman put his left hand out to meet hers. She squeezed his fingers and let go. Sizing up Friedman was easy for Vee: a bottom-line type who knows his business is star driven yet must have a good script or a big star will pass. She knew 'The Paper Man' was a damn good script and he could see that she knew it was.

—Who do you have in mind to play the Paper Man? he asked.

—Jim Carrey. Mr. Dayne won't sell the rights unless Mr. Carrey plays the lead.

—That's interesting, considering it's Mr. Dayne's first script.

She wanted to tear his head off just then, instead:

—Yes, she courtesy smiled.

—Mr. Carrey would be perfect for the part I agree..but he could be involved in other projects.

—You'll have to find that out, she said.

—Does Mr. Dayne have an agent?

—No..he represents himself.

—And if I may ask..how are you involved?

—I want to play Josie..if the chemistry is good between Mr. Carrey and myself.

—Do you have any acting experience?

—A little. Lots of training. No credits. I can do it.

Friedman began to pull at his lower lip with his thumb and index finger after leaning back in his captain's chair. As 'The Paper Man' taught her: she kept quiet, waiting for him to speak. Waiting..until:

—I suppose if Carrey's free..he could read with you.

—A screen test?

—Yes.

She could tell he was watching her from a producer's POV, gauging if this unknown Vee has a bankable face.

—Please call Mr. Dayne as soon as possible. His toll-free number and e-mail are on the script's title page. Is that about everything for now, Mr. Friedman?

—Yes, fine.

He stood and offered his right then left hand to Vee:

—Pleased to meet you, Vee.

—Yes, the same for me, she smiled.

—Sometime I'd really like to hear more about this left-handed town. Where is it?

—In Kansas.

—What's the name of the town?

—Minneapolis.

She smiled and left the office knowing she'd made a good first impression.

Once she was outside the studio gate it was easy to see Traveller parked on the street. When she opened Traveller's front passenger door she saw a slender brindle-colored Labrador/shepherd with floppy ears sitting on the front seat.

—Huck! she exclaimed.

—Surprise! Dwayne smiled from behind the wheel. Vee, could you come inside..there's someone I want you to meet. Dwayne climbed back to meet Vee and introduce her to Merry, a corpulent friendly woman from Simi Valley and owner/trainer of Lucky, the dog Dwayne hoped would play Huck in 'The Paper Man'.

—Vee, this is Merry.

—Pleased to meet you, Merry.

—I reached her on her cell phone and she dropped by with Lucky. Isn't that great!

—Yeah.

—Isn't Lucky perfect to play Huck?

We looked up front at Lucky's square snout and placid demeanor.

—He looks like a perfect match, Dwayne.

—I gave Merry a copy of 'The Paper Man' the book. She'll let us know if she can train Huck..I mean..Lucky to do all the things in the story. She thinks he can pick it all up fast. You oughtta see him beg. He's perfect, Vee.

Merry laughed, demonstrating to Vee and Dwayne:

—Lucky, Merry spoke softly.

Instantly Lucky was sitting in front of Merry waiting for her next command. To Lucky:

—Do you want something?

Lucky stood up on his hind legs, his front paws sweeping the air, his sad brown eyes begging.

—That's so perfect, Vee agreed.

Then Merry just slightly moved a finger and Lucky stopped begging, now waiting for her next pointing words:

—Now go back and sit..and speak three times.

Lucky dashed back to the passenger seat and barked three times. Merry's laugh had Dwayne and Vee laughing, knowing they found their Huck. Then Vee asked Merry if Lucky is left handed.

—Why, yes, he is! He always shakes with his left paw. I never really thought about it that way.

Vee could see Merry's chubby fingers wrapped around the cover of Dwayne's book, holding it as if she treasured this opportunity for her Lucky. Then Dwayne asked Merry how old Lucky is.

—He'll be four in November.

—That's perfect, Dwayne smiled. Perfect.

Then it hit Vee, when she saw Dwayne so happy to have found his Huck: Dwayne is the Paper Man, and he should play the role with her and Lucky. The more she thought about it, the more she could see him playing Harvey Deason. It would be nearly impossible to cast Dwayne in a leading role in this town, or to get a studio to even consider thinking about bankrolling a film with two unknowns playing the leading roles.

After Merry and Lucky left Traveller, Vee and Dwayne went to the back bedroom and hugged while falling laughing onto the bed. Still embracing, Vee kissed his neck and said:

—You found Huck! How did you find him so easily?

—I called a couple of vets in Simi Valley and one of them gave me Merry's number. I called her..and..

—What did you do when you first saw him?

—I stared in disbelief. I couldn't believe I was really seeing a dog I always imagined would play this unreal super smart dog.

—Merry seems nice, Vee said.

—She is. She said she's trained several dogs for parts in television but never for a film. She said she'd read the book and call my cell number.

—Great! Dwayne, can you really believe we're here, making this all come together.

—We have to go back to Minneapolis now..where Vicky Derryberry began her life.

—Why? You've wanted to be at this place where you can sell your work..to become a writer/in, remember? Why are you saying this now?

—I want to play Harvey in the film. But I'm not ready. I

need more time. This is your dream, too..to play Josie. But I don't trust you yet. I must trust you before I share this dream with you.

—Trust me? Trust me about what? That I won't f—— anyone but you? I'm not even divorced yet, Dwayne. It takes time to earn trust.

—It's not about that.

—Then what is it?

—Minneapolis..it's the left-handed town. And you let me drive around North Dakota knowing all the while it was your hometown. I must know more before I trust you with a story I've spent my life living, thinking and writing about. You're not just gonna f—— me and leave town with all I've invested.

—How did you find out about Minneapolis?

—When I was driving down the main drag early in the morning when you were asleep..I noticed that all the streets are one way with no right turns. I've never seen that before. I'm used to working a town and..seeing things. I noticed that all the doors to businesses and residences open to the left. And all the cursive writing on the windows in businesses are written by southpaws. And the boulders..all the streets pointed left to them after I took a left at the park and another left after the bridge. And there they were..on the left side of an open field. We have to go back now.

He flexed his fingers, extending them for her to grasp them. She hesitated, knowing she had brought him to Minneapolis, never dreaming he would discover what he had. Or, did she really know he would discover what he had because she trusted him with her dream. Soon, the yellow mist of family/past lives was coming inside Traveller.

They closed their eyes and went back, counterclockwise, this time beyond the present, not knowing if they would be together when or where they stopped.

It was the summer of 1902. It took just over a hundred years for the population of Minneapolis, Kansas to grow from 7 to 116. Joseph Bishop, his wife Agnus and their five children had made the difficult trek to Kansas in a covered wagon all the way from Boston. Mr. Bishop had only one arm, his left. He lost his right arm soon after a 2000-lb. ox fell on it when he was clearing a field. He was a right-handed man no more.

Mrs. Bishop converted to left-handedness and made sure her five children were southpaws just because she was a bit off center from sane. The Bishop neighbors got the church to castigate them for practicing such devilry, as anything related to the left was considered evil or sinister at best.

So, off the Bishops went again, with 300 dollars in savings and a full wagon pulled by a pair of oxen, one of which had caused the whole mess to begin with.

The Bishop couple were a pair made for each other it seemed. The seven strange boulders they found looming on the Kansas prairie, they believed were a sign to settle; each boulder represented a Bishop to them. In fact, each rock was named after a Bishop by them. Together they raised their five children on 70 acres of prime Kansas soil where most of Minneapolis is located today. Their homestead was named Bishopville and remained that until 1929.

Within three decades, two generations of Bishops were having more Bishops and living near the central Bishop homestead and thriving on the keen Bishop ability to create wealth by working hard and multiplication. The amazing thing: 80% of the Bishops were natural lefties and the other 20% followed suit without difficulties, except for one Bishop girl named Selina.

The Bishop children were home-schooled; and it would be hazel-eyes Selina who would be the only Bishop not to convert to being a southpaw. Even with her right arm secured to her desk by a black ribbon, Selina would do her lessons painfully slow, as if her left hand were her right, keeping her letters tall vs. the southpaws' tendency to lean them right as a forward slash.

At 14 she was caught making right-handed entries in her diary about "the abuse Bishop children endured over some silly accident involving oxen." Selina was moved into her own living quarters, a crackerbox one-room shack not far from the seven boulders. Strangely, Selina Bishop was a natural lefty, but resented the Bishop policy of forcing the left side onto her numerous siblings and cousins.

One summer night in July, soon after her 17th birthday, Selina left Bishopville for good, giving up her birthright to live her life on Bishop land that had sprawled to over 6000 acres by the summer of 1902.

She walked clear across Kansas alone until she met up with a drifter near the Colorado border. This man's name was Billy Whitehead. They first met under a railroad trestle; he was rolling a cigarette alone when she walked up to him toting two expensive suitcases that she stole from her mother's closet.

Billy, rolling a smoke under cold steel; Selina letting her bags drop to each side, this is where Vee knew she was Selina in a past life and had this connection to Dwayne, who was Billy. Only Selina knew they had this connection, just as Dwayne unconsciously knew when he met Vee in Minot.

Perhaps it was all the left-handed resistance in Bishopville and her forced mindset into being right handed that enabled her brain to become more connected, or rather, more connections to the areas of the brain that control thoughts and manifesting beliefs in thoughts to create a reality that made wealth and true love escape her. The next chapter is Billy and Selina's first meeting, written later by D. H. Dayne in 'Summer of 02'.

Selina and Billy

I can remember the first time I met her. I felt this strange feeling come over me. I call this feeling frightful/joy; it's the same feeling I always feel when I submit a novel to be read by an agent or publisher, who eventually rejects my lifelong goal and journey to become a writer/in.

I was on my ass, pinching rolling paper between my fingers while pushing tobacco onto the surface evenly. It was nearing sunset when I saw Selina coming from the east. Her hazel eyes were steady and fearless though I looked a sight worse than a dirt sandwich that smelled bad..real bad.

It was I who felt scared, when she dropped her fancy bags alongside her buckskin pants and expensive boots, and she said into my tired eyes:

—Roll one for me, too.

Then she smiled, and so did I, though she must've seen my dirty fingers trembling while she stood over me and watched me roll two fat ones that we would soon watch each other smoke for about ten minutes while we talked:

—You walkin'? I said

—Not right now.

I laughed; she said:

—I walked halfway across Kansas in nine days.

We exchanged names and quick stories how we came to bein' here. I told her I was a gypsy with no past of much interest. She told me about her family ownin' a farm and some crazy thing about all of 'em bein' left handed.

I could tell by the way she smoked that it wasn't a regular habit like with me. When she inhaled she only took it down to the bottom of her throat and blew it back out, not wanting it to go any further than that. And that was how Selina was: in control, not wanting things to go anywhere but where she wanted them to go. I liked that about her. That's why I walked with her, west, instead of no particular direction like I was used to.

For four days we walked into Colorado, the Rockies getting noticeably bigger by the start of day three. I was the one who stopped to rest more than she did. I called it a smoke break, but my feet were so sore from lousy shoes made of tough canvas and cardboard, that I welcomed any stream of mountain water to soak them in. The water would heal my body so fast–my feet felt like runnin' on rocks before puttin' on those stinky old shoes.

Selina always bought the food; we ate in restaurants mostly, but she'd buy fresh food and vegetables, enough to last us a couple days. I guess she paid my way for the protection from the bad sort of men that would prey on a woman alone on the road. In fact, I never had met an attractive woman who traveled alone like Selina did.

At night we slept on the ground under the cover of a billion silver stars. I could see her lookin' at one star at a time until her eyes closed from the fatigue of another thirty miles of road behind her. Her hair was what really was different: an auburn/gold and clean lookin' all the time even after three days between baths.

Yesterday we bathed together, instead of me with my back to her before my turn. I guess she felt safe around me once we were deep into the Rockies. If she ever knew I was aroused in the water she never let on, cause I got out with a stiff one that wouldn't go away 'til I put on those stinky shoes. I knew she saw me that way, cause the next bath time–we went back to takin' turns.

In Denver, Selina bought me a pair of good boots, soft leather ones that were tan like hers. Outside the boot store I asked her why she didn't ride a train instead of all this walkin'. She told me how she always wanted to walk to California and really see and feel the country the whole way. And she said someday, if she lived to be old, she would have a thousand memories of her walk to the golden hills of California.

For some reason, I wanted to keep walkin' with her, sometimes hopin' we never get there, because I was nothin' more than an old clump of dirty sagebrush with legs when I met Selina three weeks ago. By the time we got out of Colorado I was Billy, with good boots formed to my feet; and I was payin' attention to the road and the weather, and birds and stars, and hearin' myself laugh loud and long 'til my belly ached. Again I cared about takin' a regular bath and whether my breath smelled, though I'd never come close to kissin' her or even talkin' to her face real close to mine. The best part: she laughed her laugh. Never heard a laugh come from a woman like Selina's laugh. It was so real it made me feel ticklish all over when I'd hear it. That kind of feeling is good for any man to have. She was savin' me from my own self pity.

It wasn't 'til we reached Provo that she started to talk about that left-handed town she came from. I hadn't really said much 'bout my past 'cept that it was behind me. I s'pose a woman gets more use outta tellin' someone who'll listen. I listened:

—When I was seven years old I had a cousin who was ten years older than me. She'd sneak out at night and meet her boyfriend, a boy her age who farmed across the county with his father. A favorite spot of theirs was to lay down between three of those big boulders where nobody would see them. This one night in May a twister came down out of the sky right on these boulders, moving them around just enough to crush the two lovers to death before they even knew what happened. My cousin's father said it was God's will to take them from this earth for their carnal sins. Ever since then I started to question God, my family, and their lunacy about making every new Bishop left handed. So, I resisted them..and though I was a natural lefty..I began to do everything I could with my right hand..just to distance myself from their attempt to control who I am. Long story short: I've been saving and stealing for this walk to California for nearly ten years. When you think about running from something for that many years, everything that comes your way is special and meant to help you in some way. That's why I think of you as special, Billy. You have come into my life because you were willing to put yourself there in order for me to reach my dream. You have taken a much longer road to get here than I, Billy. Thank you.

From that moment on me and Selina became the best of friends. We settled in California, got married and had three kids.. all right handed.

That's the Spirit

After Vee read 'Billy and Selina' across from me at Traveller's booth, we went for a walk planning to stop at the retirement home where her Grandpa Derryberry has lived alone in a private room for a decade.

We stopped in the shade of the magnolias lining the river bank, which was really not much wider than a big creek with rocks and stones visible from top to bottom.

The day was turning hot with little traffic coming or going down Main. We decided to have a late breakfast in a mid-block café called Mary's Place. Before going inside, Vee explained that not everyone in Minneapolis today is left handed, that it was pretty much a thing that died in the early 20th Century after the older-generation Bishops died. And she said that the left-pointing one-way streets and such were kept pretty much the same for nostalgia.

Over breakfast we talked fast and listened good about returning from California right after finding Lucky, the perfect dog to play Huck in the script:

—I think it's about me being unable to truly give myself to one man because of holding onto past b.s.

—How are you or any of us supposed to know how to let go of any emotional connections past or present? I said.

—I heard about this woman who lived isolated for thirty years just so she could never have any new junk to carry around.

—And?

—That's it. Nobody knew of anything she did or how her life turned out.

—My bailing out in L.A. is my fear of success. I know it's somehow related to my prosperity and trusting women.

—Maybe it's a fear of love..getting and giving real love.

—I think prosperity and successful relationships are one and the same. Somehow finding you in Minot led me to this left- handed place that one-armed man in Illinois told me about last winter. And Karen charted me right to you.

—Maybe Karen can help.

—I'll call Karen later. I just think we need more time together before we take that script to L.A. Maybe we should hang in the Midwest 'til your divorce is final.

—I can't nail that script if nothing's in it for me. It'll just sit around in a box. It doesn't motivate me if we're not going to sell it. There's no way to sell a script without living in L.A., Dwayne.

—It still bothers me you didn't tell me about this place.

—I brought you here, Dwayne..for some reason.

—I understand all that. And you might be the reason my script is finally sold.

—There's something else that bothers me about our spin forward to L.A. When I was with that studio executive I told him about Minneapolis being this left-handed town where I was from. And yet I had never told you about it. It's all this past life regression from Karen's chart that keeps me close to you. It's not your script and what I can get out of it. I thought it was. But when I met Lucky..I knew that cleaning up our pasts in order to live better now is more important than some studio that wants it because they see big bucks.

—That's when I realized I should play Harvey..but I'm not ready. I'd rather have a shot at it later than blow it now.

—I understand.

—Now we're here..and I should help you find whatever you can to make your life better.

—My grandpa can help me with that. I need to go to him.

—Alone?

—No. I think I have to take him to the boulders where we found out about Billy and Selina...and the Bishops. I don't think it'll work without you there.

She put her left hand on the table. I held it with my left.

—Are we beginning again? she asked.

—Every day, I smiled.

—I want you to promise me..if I ever get self-centered to

you..you must let me know as soon as possible.

    —I will. Is there anything from this town in your experience..that you know of..I mean...

    —Are you trying to say if I know of anything that happened here to me that bothers me today?
I nodded yes.

    —Not that I know of. But that Bishop connection. If I'm related to Selina and you are related to Billy..wouldn't it be fun to follow their history?

    —Not for me. Unless I'm stuck today because of something I inherited. I understand they had a good life.

    After getting directions we walked the half-mile to the retirement home where Vee's grandfather was living. Along the way we talked:

    —What do you want to ask him? I said.

    —I want him to tell me about his life or anything he wants to tell me. And I want to know if I can learn from it..to live better somehow.

    On a hill shaped like a loaf of bread, was a brown/red brick one-story building named Prairie Home. I wished I had driven Lawn Boy and could scout around the area while Vee visited her grandpa alone. I could see her thinking about what she would say to him, and she was ruminating about their memories together on his farm when she was very young.

    As we climbed the steep driveway, a thousand such places like Prairie Home flashed in my memory from my paper man days. Herman Silver, my old Jewish boss in 'The Paper Man' was at the top. It was the last time I saw the old man alive. It was in this sterile care center in the affluent part of Woodbury. It was lunchtime. Herman's white head was slumped down to his chest, asleep in his wheelchair while three other Jewish cronies snarled at the quality of their food piled in compartments of their food trays. I sat next to Herman and patted his hunched back that was by now nearly 100 years old. He raised his head, recognized me right away and he said my name after I asked him if he remembers me.

I came out of my reverie as we reached the top of the hill; Vee was walking a step ahead of me, still thinking of her beloved Grandpa Derryberry. I stopped myself from blurting out something I saw in Herman's eyes, the old paper man. It was when we reached the Prairie Home front door I said to her after taking her hand:

—I've seen that all things happen for a reason. All of this is no accident, Vee. Do you want to be alone with him?

—I want him to meet you.
She kissed me on my lips and said to me as if she loved me:

—Thanks to you..I'm here. Thank you.
We went inside.

I told her I would only stay for a short while with her grandpa and that I wanted to go call Karen, which would give Vee private time with her grandpa. The truth: I wanted Karen to know exactly what I'm doing and where I am, in Minneapolis, Kansas where seven megalithic druid boulders stand in a field in the same town where the new love in my life is from. Karen will know.

We held hands all the way into room 117, a private room close to the middle of Prairie Home. Ralph Derryberry was seated in a straight chair with perfect ramrod posture looking out his lone window. His granddaughter stepped into the old man's line of vision while I was out of his view a few feet away. He had no idea who Vee was. She smiled into his eyes and raised her voice for him:

—Hi, Grandpa Derryberry!
She could tell he still did not recognize her and was not trying to.

—I'm Vicky..your granddaughter. Nate's daughter.
Then he smiled up at her knowing now who she was. She put her left hand on his and patted it saying so softly I could barely hear her words:

—I came here to see you, Grandpa Derryberry. How have you been?
His jaw was slack from reading her words, and it creaked from his dentures when he spoke in a forced whisper:

—Vicky...Vicky.. How are you?

—I'm fine, Grandpa. I brought a friend with me. Grandpa..this is Dwayne.

I stepped up and smiled. I offered my right hand to handshake but the old man didn't budge.

—Nice to meet you, Mr. Derryberry.

The old man smiled and shook hands when I offered my left hand.

Within five minutes: I was walking fast toward Traveller, anxious to call Karen because I thought I had a chance to dissolve some old limiting beliefs. The faster I walked–the more my brain churned out information I would examine before dismissing. The glaring fact: beliefs are specialized thought forms; beliefs determine my experiences.

Inwardly I talked, telling myself I would never have met Vee if not for Karen and her chart; I knew that my beliefs were not empowering, but rather, they were too limiting. A thousand things to ask my sister kept coming at me until I reached Traveller.

Karen was home and had time to chat with me. After I told Karen about the seven boulders I could now see outside Traveller's windows, she told me:

—When I talked to Vee she gave me her birth date and place of birth.

—Where was she born? I asked.

—Glendale, California. Dwayne, when you first went back to Ledges after that spin with Vee I did some checking on her relationship to you near Ledges and the farm. Then I plugged in the years we lived on the farm.

—And?

—Well..the lives turn to a deeper purple and a much brighter yellow.

—Like they were in Minot?

—Yeah, but not like this, Dwayne.

—What are you saying?

—I'm saying that Vee was someone we knew who lived near Ledges..in a past life.

—How do you know this?

—Karla, the woman who first told me about this chart at

the library, remember?

—Yeah.

—Well, I asked her and that's what she said. But this is the shocker.

—Karen, don't be such a drama queen. Tell me.

—Karla says it has to be someone we know who died when we lived on the farm near Ledges.

—Darlene? I said.

—That's the only person I could think of.

—No way.

—It makes sense to me, Dwayne. Darlene's last time on earth was with Mom. And she wanted to be beautiful like Mom.

—She was a little girl in Ledges when we went back. Wouldn't she have said something about being here before?

—Karla says that's the reason they return..every time..to experience the feelings they had that created their belief system.

—But you're not sure she's Darlene?

—It's not a hundred percent. Something to think about.

—Oh, yeah, something to think about..thanks Karen. Next time I'm in bed with Vee..I'll think about it.

Karen laughed hard.

—I don't know everything that's happening, Dwayne.

—That's comforting.

—When you were at Ledges with Vee she was a young girl and you were grown..right?

—Right.

—Karla says that with yellow/purple you have the universe mirroring your beliefs back to you. And it's a place on the chart that anyone should be focusing on to expand your life.

—So?

—So, you didn't want to go back and she did. Let's face it..it boils down to you going back to the farm.

—By Ledges?

—Yeah.

—Why?

—Because you were so inhibited..living in fear all the time

and unable to express your true self.

    —Are you saying if I go back to the farm with Vee we both have to be willing to go back?

    —Yes, but you have to be true and go back as Ben.

    —Ben?

    —Yeah..the way it truly was, bro.

    —Will you be there as Pam?

    —Yes.

    —So, I should tell Vee about Ben?

    —Have her read 'Ledges'. But I don't want you to go back.

    —Why? You said when I first started on your chart that this would give me another chance to express my true self and that would allow me to live a better life in the present and be a better writer that would make me a writer/in.

    —Yeah, but Darlene will be there. I'm not sure what she'll do. Did you love Darlene?

A long pause, then Karen answered:

    —I did. Show each other how you really feel.

    —And I can't change when or how she died?

    —No, you can't change the past. You can only experience what you felt..and own the feelings so you can remove those limiting thought forms that don't serve you now.

    —Why didn't you tell me these things before I met Vee?

    —Karla just told me about it, Dwayne. And you're moving around to different areas on the chart. Places are important.

    —This is all so strange, Karen..what should I do?

    —If you go back there..go somewhere first that you both know.

    —You mean me and Darlene?

    —Yeah.

    —But she's not really Darlene now.

    —No..but you'll find out if she was.

    —Did you get your check?

    —Yes, thank you.

    —Try to get me a half-dozen signings between here and

Boone. Boone and Leavenworth would be good. Find a few libraries you can schedule this week, keeping in mind I'm in Minneapolis, Kansas now. E-mail the signings to me. I gotta go. I left Vee with her grandpa at a retirement home. Oh..can you tell me what Minneapolis, Kansas reads on our charts?

I could hear Karen typing in info on her computer as she wore her phone headset. Then she told me:

—Vee's brown..very dark.

—Home and love..that fits.

—Yours is pink..passion/career. Might be a good time to do some writing, bro.

—Thanks, Karen. I love you.

—I love you, too. Call me before you get to Boone.

—I'll try. Bye.

I unhitched Lawn Boy and while driving back to get Vee I thought of all the fear, worry, doubts and judgments that tied me to my limiting beliefs back in Boone, Iowa. And would Vee even want to go back to a place where possibly she had died in a past life? And where could we go together, a place we had in common back there?

At Prairie Home, Vee was in the dining room with her grandpa; he was finished with his lunch, parked at a circular table. Vee was seated beside him. I could see she was ready to go. She wheeled him back to his room, kissed him goodbye on his cheek and squeezed his left hand while she told him that she loved him.

Once outside, she was thrilled to be out of there. She said she enjoyed her visit with her grandpa, but the stifling air mixed with the antiseptic smells and hospital food to half-dead people was tiring.

Later, riding in Traveller:

—Did he say anything interesting?

—No. After a while I could not think of anything but how I wished I was out of there..away from this town.

—Is there anyone else you want to see around here?

—No. I wish I hadn't come here now.

—Why? You got to see your grandpa.

—It just reminds me of my own mortality.

—Funny you should mention that. I want you to read 'Ledges' as fast as you can.

—A script?

—No..my novel. There's a girl in the story..Darlene..who may be related to you. Karen told me. Don't ask me why or how or anything.

I handed her a copy of the book while I drove and continued:

—We're gonna work our way back to where 'Ledges' takes place in Central Iowa. Tell me more about your visit with Grandpa Derryberry.

—It was sad. He couldn't really say much. I don't think he'll live much longer. That place is killing his spirit.

—Didn't you say he farmed his whole life?

—Yeah. So, he's really not happy to be there. Believe me. You got any sticks?

—We'll get some.

At a gas station/convenience store we bought a pack of ultra lights and smoked together outside the store. I could see her thinking hard like when we first approached Prairie Home. I said:

—This place must bring back a lot of memories.

—Isn't that all we really have in the end..when it's over?

—Yeah..maybe.

—I mean..I could see that my grandpa was holding onto some kind of memories. But mostly they were about loss. Aren't good people supposed to die peacefully with sweet content on their lips? Not this way.

—Vee, that's his choice. But what if we each died several times..and we know we didn't get it right anytime before? What if we subconsciously did know that?

—That's what I like about you, Dwayne. You know the past is always related to the present..and you don't complain about how you got here.

—Wasted energy, I laughed.

—Let's go to Ledges, she smiled.

County Fair

Library signings in Leavenworth and Council Bluffs went well, with over 60 copies of 'Shy Ann' sold in six hours. That was better than I could do on the phone..most days. Not bad for a hack, I thought.

Early August was as hot as usual in Western Iowa. Ninety-six degrees with stifling humidity 24 hours a day. Leaving Council Bluffs at noon the day after the signing there, I parked Traveller at an incredible overlook vista just off I-80.

For some reason Vee announced that her motivation died to complete 'The Paper Man' script; I knew meeting with that executive at the studio was a downer for her. Now: she had read half of 'Ledges' and met Darlene in the story. I asked her not to talk about it until she finished the book.

Via Traveller's windshield we scanned the panoramic view of the Missouri River and the green/fertile flat plains of Western Iowa and Eastern Nebraska.

—This is my home, I said.

—Not many trees around here.

—Yes, it seems that way, but there are. Will you dance with me?

She looked at me as if I was joking until I played 'Heart of Mine' by Boz Scaggs. With only the hum of the A/C after the song ended and I turned off the stereo, we continued slow-dancing in the section of space between the recliner and sofa bed. My arms were around her mid back, our waists touching as we turned counter-clockwise slow/lost in the remains of the music that has stopped. We held our eyes deep to the back of healthy hazel and weak pale blue. And for the first time in our lives together we whispered at the exact same instant:

—I love you.

We kept turning left in this slow dance that revolved much

slower than our beating hearts. For we knew this dance long ago, in another time; it was taking us back toward this atavistic spin that only we dared to welcome.

It started out real slow: in the Council Bluffs library where she sat next to him reading 'Ledges' while he signed copies of 'Shy Ann'; in Leavenworth's library while she sat at the back of the room reading 'Ledges'; Billy and Selina; the Minneapolis boulders; the first time they made love in Traveller; and their first meeting in Minot.

Meanwhile, as the dance to the left continued, they relaxed in this trusting embrace–still turning back, back, back, with their eyes closed now, spinning faster and faster into this mist of yellow/purple until: it stopped. They lost consciousness.

They awoke separated. She knows who she is and where she is. She is 14-year-old Darlene Rainbow, the wild Iowa country girl in 'Ledges' who boinked guys for cigarette money and lived in a rundown house with her parents in Boone who worked nights at a packinghouse. Darlene's body is incredible; her hair is a frizzy brown from a bad home permanent. Her face is tough looking with several scars on her face and forehead from fights with her 17-year-old step-brother Aaron and boyfriends who didn't shell out smokes or money for her services.

It's summertime, early 1960s. The Boone County Fair is opening tomorrow at the Boone Fairgrounds. Her uncle Gene was going to give her a ride to the fair but had to work some overtime in order to ready Boone school buses for the coming school year. Darlene called her neighbors at the Dutch Beal Farm a couple miles away on the other side of Ledges State Park. Pam and Ben Smith were around 10 or 11, city kids from Des Moines whose beautiful mother married Dutch Beal a few years back. Pam told Darlene on the phone yesterday that Ben was going to give her a ride on his bike. Darlene said to stop by on the way and she'd ride her uncle's bike with them to the fair.

Just before bedtime, Pam got in trouble with Dutch for eating all the ice cream, so Dutch told her she couldn't go to the fair. Pam was not too disappointed, since the ride side-saddle on her brother's bike was painful for her leg and lower back, not to mention all the walking on the fairgrounds.

Ben feared that if he went to Darlene's alone she might try to force him to smoke, fool around, steal cigarettes from the Boone IGA, or force him to dance with her at the fair because the Everly Brothers are performing there.

Ben hated wearing his Buddy Holly glasses when he rode his bike. The lenses would never fail to fog from perspiration around his eyes. He had to wear them because he was as blind as Hutch without them. Ben's red Super Chief with whitewalls was his most treasured possession.

His ride through Ledges changed from sweat-making heat to massive cool pools of shade splashed with these mere slits of goldenrod sunshine, light that was able to filter to earth through the thickest of foliage and the oldest trees in Iowa. Ben has no recall of who he may become, only that he was stunted emotionally. A ten-year-old boy should bounce in and out of his feelings, observing them without judgment. But Ben had put himself in the middle, not allowing joy or sadness to ride along his path. Fear would be the lesson, always: fear of joy and fear of loss.

Except for his sister Pam, Ledges was his best friend. He would come here to hide his bike and lope along the endless miles of trails, sometimes talking out loud to other things and sounds made from the park. Mostly, Ben would talk about how he felt scared for doing something his step-dad didn't like, and would scold himself for feeling that way. Stuffing it down, he called it; in fact he was so good at it–many times his heart stayed calm during dangerous times: the forgotten water tank filled for the cattle; a broken or lost tool; and the most terrifying: those fears of the unknown, and unable to voice or ask for an explanation from a strong middle-aged man who shared none of his bloodline, yet slept in his mother's bed.

His mother called it 'tough love' and said that it's better to be disciplined and learn from a smart man than to be on your own in a brutal world of hard knocks learned from strangers.

The narrow winding road until the heart of Ledges was but quarter-mile, yet in that time of perhaps a couple hundred revolutions on his cherry red Super Chief-the terrible sounds and visions in his head would cease, to be replaced with birds in song and flight, in colors he'd only seen on Ledges flowers. He thought the birds got their colors from the very seeds of the flowers they consumed.

A knee-deep stream that ran alongside the road was overflowing, spilling across the road and falling loud off the other side of the road. Ben raised his legs to rest atop his chrome handlebars and coasted through the water for twenty yards without getting his shoes or jeans wet. When he pedaled again, Darlene's image was racing his heart as if he'd just sprinted through the park without stopping. So many times Darlene had intimidated him and his sister during their ride on the school bus just by being the free spirit she truly was for 24 hours a day. Even the way she chewed her gum-smacking her lips and popping tiny bubbles on her back teeth that they could hear above the roar of the Blue Bird's mighty engine that her Uncle Gene drove so adroitly.

And he saw her remove her used gum from her mouth, roll it into a ball and plaster it under her reserved seat across from her uncle, then Ben saw her retrieve the 7-hour-old wad of gum after school on her ride home. It was the way she retrieved it that he would always remember, without her showing the slightest trace of self-consciousness. Never would she look or even care if anyone saw her going after that old wad of gum under the seat.

That kind of freedom or lack of self-consciousness is what Ben wanted, even more than he wanted his precious bike that now brought him to the back entrance to the park, a half-mile from Darlene Rainbow's house. Here is where weeds grew tall on both sides of the gravel road with leaves like elephant ears that Ben knew oozed a milky liquid when cut with a machete.

Darlene could hear Ben's bike coming down the road outside her open front door that she left open to let the flies out. She was on her twin-sized bed, half asleep and naked under pastel yellow cotton sheets that were damp from the humidity and weeks of body sweat that was not all hers.

Summer was Darlene's time to forget time. She'd lie in bed 'til two or three in the afternoon after staying up all night watching TV and smoke her parents' Pall Mall non-filters. Her parents, Ray and Charlotte slept in the big bedroom until 7 PM, then would get up, get dressed, take their dirty smocks to a Boone Laundromat, eat and have a few beers at Roscoe's Tap before driving 89 miles to work graveyard at a Denison packinghouse where they'd end their shift every morning after their only hot showers in the plant locker rooms. Most weekends, if they didn't work overtime, they'd sleep in on their king-sized tomb shrouded in darkness until they'd get up and prepare for a late night at Roscoe's.

She hears his kickstand scrape across her concrete front porch. She began to giggle while thinking of cute Ben Smith in those big/thick black glasses with his blonde flat-top spiked evenly above the top of his forehead.

—Benny, she giggled out loud as she curled toward her open bedroom door with only her jagged toothy grin showing above the covers.

She giggled again when she heard his timid call for her from the open front door. Silence. She wanted him to come into her room.

His glasses were steaming, giving him an even gloomier view of the Rainbow interior. Ashtrays overflowed everywhere with crushed butts; a herd of black houseflies dined on rings of dried ham bones left on paper plates on the diningroom table; pop cans and plastic drinking glasses were scattered on furniture of dirty orange, a matching sofa and chair stained from a thousand spills; a brown recliner was covered with a dingy white sheet to hide the tears taped with gray electrical tape; the carpet: a disgusting rust-colored shag with bits of dropped food everywhere, mostly popcorn; a color TV held framed color photos of relatives and Darlene's 6th grade picture.

When he walked, the smells of old cigarette smoke and fried foods were soaked into the once-white walls now stained yellow. Even flies collected on wall space as if to lick grease from them. A white cat the size of a beagle peered at Ben from Darlene's dark

bedroom entrance. He thought he heard her giggling..again after h
called her name. He blushed while holding his breath when he
turned to see that Ray and Charlotte's bedroom door was closed an
that they must be sleeping.

He knocked lightly on Darlene's open bedroom door after
wiping the fog from his lenses. He could barely make out her face
in the darkness.

—Hi, Benny! she laughed. Oh my God! she screamed. The
fair! I forgot!

She popped out of bed so fast he could hardly believe his weak
eyes. Besides his sisters and his mother, Darlene Rainbow was the
first girl he'd seen naked. And what a body. Her figure was that of
a grown woman with no tan lines. She was thoroughly tickled to
see Ben's red face at her doorway when she turned on the overhead
light in her messy room. His eyes went to the floor, to the clutter o
dirty clothes that would fill three washing machines.

When she found a pair of jean cut-offs on the floor, he
watched her put them on with her back to him. Her legs and
buttocks were brown and muscular. Then: she turned to him
quickly, knowing she would catch his eyes darting away from
behind his thick glasses. He was too afraid to ask her what he felt
he wanted. Older boys by the score he had seen come and go from
this house day and night. What she gave them–he, too, wanted.

—Benny, I can't go to the fair 'til I clean the house, she
smiled as she put on a sleeveless white T-short. I was gonna do it
last night..but I got back too late from the drive-in movie. If my
parents wake up and find a mess..they'll ground my ass.

—I'll help ya.

—Really?

She thought he was cute, this virgin boy with nice clean
clothes from a rich family. Darlene raked every piece of clothing
off the floor in her room and carried them to the back porch laundry
area as Ben got a paper sack from the kitchen and started filling it
with garbage in the front room.

—You got a vacuum?

—In the closet, she pointed while filling the kitchen sink

with hot dishwater.

—Won't it wake up your parents?

—No..they don't hear nothin' in there. They wear earplugs when they sleep.

He never vacuumed such a messy carpet as the Rainbow's. Dozens of coins would rattle when sucked from the deep shag; white cat hair wrapped around popcorn; bobby pins and bottle caps; cigarette butts and gum wrappers; and a thousand other things that God only knows.

Darlene worked fast going from table to table wiping with the same dishrag she would use to wash the dishes. Then: Ben's eyes began to burn when she shut the front door and sprayed every inch of air space with bug spray. Before long, Ben's eyes were so irritated he had to go outside and spray the garden hose directly into his red eyes. When he dropped the hose to the new mud under his feet he saw the faded-silver little house trailer where Gene Rainbow lived. Gene was Darlene's uncle and their bus driver to school and back. Ben could see that Gene's bike and car were gone from their usual parking spots.

Blink after blink he made his way to Gene's trailer. He turned the trailer's only doorknob. It opened. He could see Darlene's back to him on the back porch as she shoved her dirty clothes into a running washing machine that didn't work half the time.

Gene's home was Spartan clean, a refreshing oasis of frugal order compared to Darlene's pigpen. He stood on a green oval welcome mat with Gene's front door closed and against his back. His eyes roamed left to right across the front room to the kitchen on his right. Muscle spasms fired in his lower back when he squinted to see the four days of the fair on a John Deere wall calendar. Right now, he'd rather be alone here than alone with Darlene in her house. Behind him he heard a familiar sound: the wheels of his Fire Chief crunching gravel.

She didn't say anything about Ben being inside her uncle's trailer, and he didn't say no when Darlene said she would pedal from the seat while he rode side-saddle and steered them to the fairgrounds.

The county road was small gravel and flat with no turns for most of the ride. Darlene kept her strong hands akimbo while her muscular legs pedaled them faster than Ben could've.

—How come Pam didn't come?

—She got in trouble with Dutch for eating all the ice cream. To his surprise, from her red/white scarf blouse pocket, a top that exposed her flat brown belly, she pulled out a Pall Mall and lit it, puffing away as she pedaled. She offered Ben the west end of the non-filter near his left ear:

—Wanna drag, Benny?

He nodded no, pursing his lips tight, steering them into a pothole:

—Watch it, Benny! That's hard on my ass!

When they crossed the highway, Ben's back was killing him from being hunched forward and twisted with his arms spread out. Once, he sat up straight to relieve his back and Darlene pressed and rubbed her boobs into his back when asking him how much money he has for the fair:

—Ten dollars.

—Ten bucks! Damn, Benny..that's ten more bucks than I have! Can we stop at the drugstore on the way? I wanna get some cigs.

Now: it was embarrassing to be the boy and steering for the girl when they reached downtown Boone. From the big window in front of Boone Drug he watched Darlene steal a pack of smokes out of a carton without being seen.

When she came back outside she was pepper-smacking one end of the Pall Malls on her wrist. She lit one and sat with her firm rump on the sidewalk against the front of the drugstore under the shade of a green and white striped canvas awning. From about six feet away, standing and arching his sore back Ben watched her smoke, inhaling deep and splitting the exhale between her nose and mouth, then again out her nose.

—When did you start smoking? he asked.

—I was about eight or nine, she recalled. Yeah..eight or nine.

—You smoke in front of your parents?

—Oh, yeah. They say they started smoking when they were young, too. Benny?

—Yeah?

—Can I ask ya somethin'?

—I don't care.

—Are you a virgin?

She knew the answer from his quick blush, and then his answer while his eyes averted down when she told her he's only ten. She laughed. Not to tease him. He tickled her in her usual crude manner.

—I got crabs once, she said, then laughed at the thought of telling this to a straight city boy.

—What are crabs? he asked.

—They're little bitty crabs that you get on yer hair down there, she pointed. They itch more on guys. I got 'em from my brother Aaron. We're not blood related.

—You still have 'em?

—No..I brushed 'em out with kerosene. That was the last time I was with Aaron. He's always got 'em. He gets 'em from nigger girls in Kansas City.

From her front pocket Darlene pulled out a plastic bag of white powder and shook it at Ben a few times.

—What's that? he asked.

—Alum. It's stuff that makes yer lips pucker like crazy, she demonstrated. And ya can hardly say a word if yer lucky. I'm gonna put it in Donna Reasoner's lemonade. She's the Boone County Queen.

—Why?

—Cuz she thinks she's hot stuff..Miss Perfect. I just wanna see her lips pucker like this when she has to kiss all those dumb boys who pay her a dollar a kiss at the kissin' both.

—That's mean, Ben laughed.

—I don't care if it is..I'm gonna do it.

—Why?

—She's always makin' fun of me and my Uncle Gene.

—Because of the way he shakes his head?

—Yeah. And she's always got her nose turned up 'round me..like I'm some pile of shit on two legs..compared to her.

—I'll walk the rest of the way if ya go slow, he said.

—Don't you wanna ride? I'll steer..you can pedal.

—No..my back hurts. I'll walk.

Darlene smoked while she rode Ben's bike on the sidewalk. Ben walked fast, though Darlene stopped and stuttered many times until they hit the road that ran north to the fairgrounds. Traffic was getting heavy and backed up three blocks from the fairgrounds entrance. Darlene stayed behind Ben on the right shoulder. She surprised him:

—Benny, would you pay a buck to kiss me?

—I don't think I'd pay a buck to kiss anybody.

She laughed, unable to tell that Ben's neck was on fire.

—Have you ever kissed a girl, Benny?

—No.

—Wouldn't you pay one measly dollar to kiss that Miss Perfect Queen Donna Reasoner?

—No.

—Would you pay a buck to see her naked body?

—Maybe, Ben confessed.

—Would you pay a buck to see my naked body?

Now: is one of those moments Ben Smith has always been too scared to enjoy. Something about doing anything secret or out of the norm terrified him. Darlene wasn't going away. She repeated the question and pedaled even with his gait, looking for his answer on his blushing face. As she giggled, his face reddened until he thought blood would burst from his ears.

She rode ahead a few feet then braked hard, turning the red Fire Chief sideways, blocking Ben's way while facing him with those muscular brown legs and bare feet poised to move the bike into his path if he tried to go around her.

—Benny..for the rest of yer long life..you'll always wonder what you would've seen for one lousy buck. Is it worth it? Or..are you scared?

—I'm not scared, he growled.

—Good..then after the Everly Brothers we'll go into Ledges..when it's dark. I know a good place.

—It'll be dark.

—Yer light works..don't it?

She got off his bike, lit a cig and pushed his Fire Chief over to him.

—Give me the buck now..so I can buy a corn dog and a cold pop.

When he handed her a dollar she kissed him quick on his cheek.

—You can ride it, she said. My ass is sore.

Darlene ran down the shoulder yelling back to Ben that she'd meet him at the concert, again flaming his face and ears crimson. The bike's seat was hot from Darlene's energy. He felt ill, as if he just betrayed his family. Ben knew that if his sister Pam ever got wind of paying Darlene Rainbow a buck to see her naked-she'd tell their mother as fast as she could.

He pedaled in a daze, passing under the paper fairground entrance banner of red and gold, knowing full well Darlene would tell his sister all the details. There was no doubt about that in Ben's mind. And that would be the end of his reign as Prince Ben, the pleaser of guardians and absolute ruler of his two sisters. It would also change his life to the carnal, wanting more and more of Darlene until he was one of her regular boys.

After he chained his bike to a post close to Gene's old Plymouth he could see his future: he would smoke with her and sneak in and out of her dirty house just to touch and explore every inch of that perfect naked body; Darlene and his sister would tease him on the bus to and from school; classmates would label him one of 'Darlene's boys' who smoke and who boink her. And the crabs: Dutch his step-dad would drown him in kerosene and kick his butt around the farm until his butt was gone. His mother would never again see the proud son whom she trusted to keep her proud of him. Instead, his mother would see a buck-toothed smoker with thick glasses who carried the sweat of a whore on his loins, and the vacuous eyes of a Darlene's boy who was ruined because he was taught carnal pleasures when he was far too young.

The biggest reason to stay away from Darlene was coming toward him wearing butterscotch-rimmed sunglasses with forest green lenses that shaded and concealed the constant pain in his moving eyes.

—Hi, Gene!

Gene's smile was one that showed no teeth, only thin lips curved upward. It was genuine despite being in constant motion. Gene's simian blonde head had a negative nod, back and forth, a kind of palsy that looked as if he was always saying no with his head.

People around Boone were used to him and didn't stare. Everyone around this part of Iowa knew that he hardly ever spoke—unless he really liked you. He liked Ben.

—Hi, Ben! Wh..where's P..Pam?

—She couldn't come. I rode my bike with Darlene. I steered and she pedaled.

—And smoked? Gene smiled.

—Yeah, Ben stopped himself from nodding yes in sync with Gene's no. What are you doing here, Gene?

He watched his driver's words come out slow and drawn out in bursts of trapped air:

—Con..con..cessions. And..and..helpin' Ev..Everly Brothers set up.

Gene pointed at Ben's bike and went over to it stroking dust from the chrome front fender as if the bike was an animal to be cared for. When Gene knelt as if to see the Fire Chief from a boy's point of view, Ben could see these tiny white hairs on the back of Gene's neck below his butch-style hairline in restless motion.

He wondered how Gene could ever get his hair cut by that elderly Boone barber who seemed to cut every man's hair in the county. Just then:

—Whatcha doin'? Darlene smiled while sucking her corn dog and holding a paper cup of iced Coke.

She offered Ben a drink of her pop.

—No, thanks.

Ben thought it sort of beautiful how relaxed and unselfconscious she was with her feet so mud-caked then dried to a crusty gray/brown dirt around her toes and the sides of her flat brown feet that appeared bigger because of her jagged toenails that had these flakes of passion pink polish on them.

It was then that Ben became self-consciously aroused when he could see her nipples visible behind her white sleeveless T-shirt. And he could see that pack of stolen Pall Malls wedged between her cut-offs and flat belly that gave her an incredibly sexy look until he got to her face and could see the only attractive feature on it–her total absence of self-consciousness.

When she knelt beside her uncle to offer him a drink of her pop, Ben could see she was not wearing any underwear. It was amazing to see how she knew just how to put the rim of the cup to her uncle's lips in motion, going with the movement of the neck and tipping it ever so slowly without spilling a drop.

When she lit a cig with both knees on the ground, Gene appeared to not care the slightest bit.

—Me and Ben will ride his bike back after the concert. The light works real good..so that'll be real fun.
Gene wiped clean, with his palm, the red plastic reflector on the bike's back fender.

—You be careful, Gene muttered to his niece.

—We will.
Darlene kissed the side of Gene's neck under his red baseball cap and whispered something to him that Ben could not hear.

Locals were filing in, going from booth to booth. There was a 4-H pen with a prize bull; a pink sow the size of a hippo; cotton candy and hot dog vendors on wheels; colorful pennants advertising Iowa products and landmarks; a local leather manufacturer displayed hundreds of belts like snakes dangling from hooks; a canvas tent that smelled of hickory, covered dozens of picnic tables for a massive barbeque feed and beer bust; and, there was Donna Reasoner's booth, the new queen, sitting behind a table under a pink umbrella, waiting to be kissed for a dollar.

There was no lemonade or a beverage of any kind near her. To spike her lips with alum appeared impossible to Darlene. Boone boys, mostly 15 to 19, were lined up for a quick kiss on the lips of

Miss Perfect, a Donna Reed clone without the talent. Darlene became angry and jealous when she saw Ben staring at the buxom blonde from Webster City, his buck teeth protruding as if he were seeing Donna Reed herself.

—Why don't ya take a picture, Benny?

Ben blushed and walked away, over where his bike was parked. He hoped Gene was still there.

She watched him leave, knowing she had embarrassed him because of the two boys that laughed at her comment.

—What a pussy, she said out loud.

She watched 'her majesty' kiss a dozen boys; at least two of them did more than kiss Darlene Rainbow more than once for a pack of smokes. It bothered her that she scared off Ben. She was thinking of the boys she boinked then kicked out of her house before Gene came over or her parents got up. None of them were as nice or as cute as Benny, she mused.

Gene was setting up the stage for the Everly Brothers when Darlene asked her uncle if he'd seen Ben. He gave a thumbs down.

—His bike's gone. Can I borrow yer car?

Gene wished he could tell her "Do I look stupid to you?"; instead, another thumbs down. But Gene pulled out his car keys from his front pocket and displayed his trunk key saying that his bike was in the trunk.

She pedaled fast, standing up until the old red bike's wheels allowed her to maintain a speed she believed was above Ben's ability to reach. Thrilled to be a tomboy, she welcomed this change of pace, hunting down a city boy whom she could dominate and control and not have the slightest chance of getting crabs. A virgin, she laughed, until she reached the downtown Boone railroad tracks. If she caught up to him, she thought about another place they could go to near Ledges, a place that was safe and clean: Uncle Gene's trailer.

Darlene never caught Ben. It truly was all a dream for me and Vee when we came back to the present in Traveller at that incredible viewing spot in Western Iowa. And yet: it wasn't our dream at all.

Vee started to cry when I played 'When the Hunter Gets Captured by the Game', the same song I played in Minot when we first met. I took her in my arms and slow-danced with her beside Traveller's booth. She cried on my shoulder, digging her chin into my flesh.

—It wasn't my dream or yours..was it? she asked.
I nodded no and continued nodding until she picked up on it:
—Gene? she said.
I nodded yes.
—How do you know? she asked.
—Darlene died young. She was killed in a car/train accident. Ben never went with Darlene to any county fair. I know now it had to be Gene's dream..after he lost Darlene.
—Was I Darlene..in a past life?
—I can't say for sure.
—Were you Ben?
—Yes.
The song ended. I turned off the CD player with the remote.
—I don't get it. Why were we in Gene's dream?
—I don't know. I know I have to see Gene again. It's important to me that you finish 'Ledges' soon.
—Okay.
—I know I would not be experiencing this alone. Alone, I'd be wandering from town to town selling books day after day. I used to think I'd find a perfect girl for me in this perfect little town..and in every way we'd be perfectly happy.
—'It's a Wonderful Life'.
—Yeah..just like Jimmy Stewart. In reality, I'd be alone sitting on benches describing trees and people and Main Streets around me. I'd always be the stranger in town. Then Karen plugged me into this chart she created..and here you are..going back to visit these characters I wrote about in these places years ago. I haven't really given Karen the whole story about what we experienced together. I'm afraid it will go away. I believe emotions we carry from our past determines who we become.

That's how we are all related.

Vee looked at him and could see that something had changed about his face since returning from the fair. She asked him if he could see anything different about her since then. He looked..but only saw beauty..no changes, except:

—You appear..less fearful. Your eyes seem more intelligent.

—I feel closer to you, she smiled.

—Maybe that's it..but I know from experience that each time I release emotions from the past I remove a layer that kept me from reaching my potential.

—We must have thousands of these layers.

—We do. That's why we're always living with this mask that's even covering our vital organs. We're constantly living with our past in the present..and our future depends on these emotions we choose to hold onto. That's why I have to find Gene. He's the only person I ever met who I saw transform his life by totally letting go. The last time I saw him he was so clear..his eyes were like these crystal white/blue marbles that used to be so pinched with painful emotions.

—I'll finish 'Ledges' as fast as I can.

—I'll drive us to Boone..while you read.

Storm Over Ledges

It took two hours to drive Traveller to the old Beal farm that was now owned by Luther Olson, a 70-year-old bachelor who had farmed six miles south of here.

Vee finished 'Ledges' not long before I parked Traveller on Olson's central farmyard. It was dark now. When Vee came to the front she knew where she was. It was like she had spun back again in time to this place I had described exactly as it is now. I didn't ask her about the story. We exited Traveller from different doors.

An old collie barked a few times from the back porch, then stopped. The dog didn't move toward us because of bad hips. There were no lights on in the white two-story farmhouse. We held hands by the same light pole in the middle of the farmyard. I could see Vee looking at me as if to gauge my reaction to being here. She wanted to explain how surreal this is, being here now after just reading 'Ledges'; instead we listened to the chirping insects that seemed to be sending their noise on these air waves saturated with incredibly high humidity.

We turned left, together, scanning the farm the way Ben had in 'Ledges' on his first visit to the farm nearly forty years ago: the outhouse, where Pam was so frightened of wasps; Dutch's shop, where he worked on his machinery. Then Vee pointed:

—There's the chicken coop..and the hog yard where Ben and Pam chased the pigs. Did that really happen here to you?

My eyes were on the dark outline of Ben's 'high place', a corn crib that was the tallest building on the farm. Then, I told Vee:

—I don't want to say this, that or the other happened here. Even when I wrote about the things that did happen I didn't remove or move the same emotions that I felt at the time they happened. Most people think that writers are good at self therapy for resolving issues. But the damn things stay with you after you write them down. I write to validate I was here..that I existed..instead of a life unlived.

—Then why are we here? she asked.

I looked away from her hazel glow and back to the high place, then back to her eyes when I said:

—To see Gene..talk to him about his life..and to find out if he could know if you were Darlene in a past life. Maybe I could sell some books here..hopefully. And to possibly let go of old emotions that we carry around with us today.

When Vee kissed my cheek a pair of headlights were coming toward us from the front road and parked in front of the house.

—That's where Ernie's cab was parked when Pam blew up Hutch.

—Did that..., she stopped herself from asking.

I smiled into her eyes as we held hands and waited for the man approaching. I waved at him and yelled "Hello!". Vee laughed and waved with her free hand, saying cynically:

—I'm not yellin' hello. God I'm craving a smoke.

The old farmer, dressed in clean jeans, royal blue T-shirt and dress boots, walked past his tail-wagging collie who now barked only twice as his master headed for the two strangers.

—Mr. Olson? I said.

—Yes!

Mr. Olson wore these brown smoke-tinted lenses and was twirling a toothpick between two back teeth when he got close enough to see that we were strangers to him. The old man was friendly and loose as if he'd had a few drinks. He extended his right hand into mine:

—My name's Dwayne Dayne and this is Vee. I used to live here a long time ago. We were drivin' by..and thought we'd stop.

—Ya brought yer house with ya I see, Olson smiled.

—Yeah, saves on motels, I smiled.

—That's a nice one, he said while his eyes darted over Traveller.

—I hope it's not a problem..just stopping by like this, Vee said.

—No..lucky I came home from the VFW early.

—How long have you lived here? I asked.

—Oh..'bout seventeen years. Would ya like to come inside, have some coffee?

—Sure! we both said together.

Vee was apprehensive about the collie after just finishing 'Ledges.' But we passed without incident, the dog too old and arthritic to muster any aggression. Vee was more anxious than me to tour the house when Olson offered.

On the main floor she made comments about things related to the book:

—This looks so familiar, just like you described it. That looks like Dutch's recliner. This was Ben's room. There's the front porch.

It was on the second floor when I felt something, a shift from an unconscious memory sensation that made this bubble-popping sound at the back of my neck. It was when I stepped into the hallway as Vee and Mr. Olson continued down the hall after Vee had pointed out the mysterious locked room that was now unlocked and used for storage. I wondered just how powerful emotions can be while I remained still and waited to see if my memory gave me an image or anything.

Nothing. Until I went to the bedroom windows in Pam and Debi's room. It was there in the glass reflection behind me: Vee's perfect body standing where Darlene had danced with my sisters. In the book, Ben was not here at that time. In reality: Ben danced with Darlene while his sisters laughed from the bed with the music playing so very loud from our mother's portable blue stereo. I mumbled:

—Blue stereo.

—What? Vee asked.

—Blue stereo. I called my mother's record player blue stereo because of the sad torch songs she'd play on it.
I stopped myself from saying more, for I could see that Mr. Olson was confused and might feel left out of the tour.

—Coffee sounds good.

As we tramped downstairs I heard the same creaking wood underfoot, though it was now carpeted with the thickest carpet possible.

In the kitchen, over coffee, all things appeared smaller to me compared to the last time I was here when I was nine. Nice Mr. Olson sat at the head of his square oak table with its matching four chairs. I could see that the wood was worn on his chair as if he ate alone most of his 17 years here. He appeared to be directing his husky voice to Vee as we listened to his plaintive stories of his life, the life before he lived here.

It was a life filled with working the everlasting land and neighbors long gone–all told with these deep smiling lines on his weather-beaten face and those bulging red eyes fresh from the VFW. As beautiful Vee politely nodded and listened with her incredible hazel eyes my eyes would dart to the little things that I was trained to notice: the single knife, fork and spoon and white porcelain plate in the yellow dish rack; the absolute feeling of aloneness that dripped and oozed from ceiling to floor, from wall to wall; and that same feeling seemed to be riding on the very sound waves that were used to leaving his dry lips and dying before any human ear heard them.

And then this overwhelming feeling hit me hard. This poor hard-working man, so alone in his solid house-would be me if not for Vee. For some thirty minutes I watched Vee listen to the farmer, wondering why on earth would she be here on some obscure piece of land when she could be wining and dining in L.A. or NYC with any man from any station in life; she could be getting closer to her dream of becoming an actress.

Though I had amazingly found Huck in L.A., the perfect dog to play the sales-collared sidekick of The Paper Man, she never put up the slightest challenge to my decision to walk away from tinsel town. In three weeks I would return her to Minot, when she would be officially free again. If this was but a summer tryst: "I'll take it," I told myself.

I caught her eye during an overhead stretch that told her I wanted to ditch outside for a smoke.

—I'll go have a smoke with you, she said as she stood with me and stretched.

—Mr. Olson, would you mind if we parked overnight here and walked around yer farm in the morning? I asked.

—Sure! Stay as long as you like. Got plenty of space, he winked at Vee.

I got the pack of sticks and some matches from Lawn Boy's dash. We smoked under the moonless sky with stars much brighter and far easier to see up there. Vee watched the frenzied millers and bugs dance around the pole light.

—Lots of bugs out here, she said.

—Yeah.

—What's it like for you to be here now? I mean..after reading 'Ledges' you really went through some heavy shit here.

—When we were upstairs I saw your reflection in the window. It reminded me of when I danced with Darlene there.

—Pam and Debi danced with her there, too.

—Yeah. That was such a rush to feel the thrill of dancing with her again..just for a moment.

—Could we go back again..spin back from here? she asked.

—I don't know..maybe. It just happens.

—There's so much I'd like to ask you..about 'Ledges'..but I get the impression you don't want to talk about it.

—It's fiction, Vee..with elements of truth. I don't want to pick out every little fact in a story that doesn't really mean shit in the real world. I fact..I'm surprised and elated that I can even be here without feeling old emotions. It means I've let go of it. If I was feeling stuff..I'd tell ya..to help dissolve it.

She nodded that she understood and squeezed the back of my neck, and said softly:

—Maybe tomorrow we can find Gene.

—Maybe.

We went to bed holding each other under the open window that wafted in the smells of a typical Iowa farm.

—I used to have hay fever here really bad this time of year..day and night.

—I read that, Vee laughed.
I pulled her closer to me and laughed in her hair before I said:
—While you were talking to Mr. Olson I was thinking how lucky I am to have you with me..and..I wondered how long it would last. She turned her face to mine and kissed the tobacco taste on my lips, saying:
—Is my breath as bad as yours?
After a long laugh for both of us we brushed our teeth before making love in Traveller's bedroom under the pole light in Farmer Olson's central farmyard.

Vee was asleep first. I even thought her snore was beautiful. I was getting close to drifting off to sleep to those sounds of insects creaking and chirping in a thousand near places that would or never could be discovered. Sounds that prove they are out there..yet "unfindable" and elusive as the very emotions we all carry for a lifetime. Until sleep came I whispered to myself:
—Emotions are the key.

Next morning: Vee woke up in Traveller's bed alone. There were no sounds coming from beyond the open bedroom door. She thought Dwayne was writing as she hurried out of bed naked to the kitchen. He was nowhere in Traveller. She brushed her teeth and remembered her dream during the night while she put her clothes on fast.

She had dreamed that she had made love to Dwayne in Ledges State Park at a secret place. She thought she had the dream because of Darlene and Ben in 'Ledges' and Dwayne's memory of dancing with Darlene.

When Vee exited Traveller and stepped down to the hard dirt, the air here was heavier than any humidity she'd ever experienced. But this was not the central farmyard on Mr. Olson's farm where they were parked last night. The trees looked familiar to her.
—Ledges, she whispered.
Then she called for Dwayne, but no answer. She wondered if this was the present as her heart beat faster. Could this be part of a

spin..back to Ledges? she asked herself. Or had Dwayne driven here while she slept and he went for a walk in the park?

Traveller was the only vehicle in sight. She looked and saw that Lawn Boy was still in tow. Down the narrow main road she walked, feeling certain she would have remembered or felt Traveller moving even though she was a sound sleeper. For some visceral inchoate reason she wanted to yell for Dwayne before she reached the first turn. Just before the bend she looked back and Traveller was now gone.

Since Ledges is so verdant this time of year she couldn't see any sky until fifty more yards. Then: she looked up and knew they had to be in one of those spins, because the sky was red with a black storm behind the red that appeared ready to unleash something awfully bad.

On her right, a running stream was but the only sound in incredible Ledges State Park. She went to the water, bending with ease when she got a handful of water to splash on her face. It was crystal green cold water. Suddenly: the stream stopped running. Her reflection was not her. This face had blemishes and scars with brown eyes and frizzy brown hair.

—Darlene, she mumbled.

She felt her breasts that were now larger and firm. Then she unzipped her cut-offs and could not find her red heart tattoo. And she was barefoot. She could not remember leaving Traveller with no shoes on her feet. Her legs felt strong, like they could climb anything with the prowess of a big cat. In her back pocket was a flattened pack of Pall Malls that had only one cigarette left in it along with a book of matches. She lit it and craned her head upward to the massive sandstone ledges. At the highest point she saw an outline of two people sitting together. She waved. Both waved back.

Darlene climbed step after step made of sturdy railroad ties salted with sand from the river. She butted her last smoke on a timber and returned it and the matches into the package.

—Benny! she called. I'm comin'!

To see Ben was always a thrill for Darlene Rainbow, and

even when she sat across from him and his sister Pam on Gene's bus. But to see these two together now had this calming effect on Darlene that she rarely experienced. Their backs were to her. Her decision to sit next to Ben brought a smirk from her Uncle Gene, his head nodding slowly, a sign to her that he was relaxed and out of the public eye.

Ben noticed that her thighs were bigger, stronger and more tan than his. From here, all three now focused on the red sky over Ledges. Gene's words were forced and foreboding:

—This storm will flood the park.

They stood up with Gene and followed him down the steps; that's when the first drops of rain fell from the red sky. These were big raindrops that tasted sweet to Darlene; they foretold of lessons in family/past lives that can only be imagined or felt by the same invisible forces that have the power to create Ledges.

They followed Gene's long simian strides, conscious strides that avoided puddles, rocks, the deeper mud, and the endless places of earth that sustained flowers of every imagined color. Every flower and weed, vine and tree, was a living thing to Gene Rainbow. Because of his constant head motion from side to side, like windshield wipers with two speeds, the slower the swipe–the more calm Gene was. So his eyes missed nothing. All living things in the park revealed things to him that others couldn't see. Like the black-tailed squirrel that pranced down the trail ahead of Gene, stopping every 20 feet or so to look back at him as if he was not a stranger, but rather, a two-legged friend who found him starving inside a broken branch last October. A friend who brought him milk every day for 29 days until he was able to shop alone in Ledges.

Yes, Gene Rainbow knows that the storm over Ledges comes every six years on the average. Never has he been caught under the red sky..until now with Darlene and Ben trusting his lead. They were going east to a part of the park that never flooded, following the same trail that Native Americans took when the 'great water' came. Some of these places in the park closer to the river were flooded under 20-feet-plus of water.

Rain came down harder and harder. Ben was at the back of the trio trying to stay close to Darlene without breathing too hard, not wanting her to think he was the same weak city boy who was always intimidated by her on the bus.

The bus: that's where Gene was leading them, to the abandoned Blue Bird school bus made in Mitchell, Indiana that Gene had parked just outside the east border of Ledges. He parked it there, with permission, on Gerald Frisbee's land, wanting to someday convert it to a motor home.

Ben remembered Darlene telling him that Gene would practice sitting behind the wheel of the old bus, using all the mirrors and getting familiar with the gear shift–the feel of being a bus driver.

Orange rust was the color if its exterior now.

—How come we didn't go home, Uncle Gene?

He didn't answer, because the rain was too loud, and the bus door was gone.

They stepped up into the front with Gene sitting on the driver's seat. Darlene took her usual spot: the front seat near the open doorway. Ben sat across from Darlene, where he and his sister Pam sat on Gene's route to and from school.

Nobody said a word for at least a minute; they sat in their space listening to the rain pounding like marbles machine-gunning the roof of the old bus. One would have to yell to even be heard above the din.

Gene was like a cat wearing his old gray bus pants when he got up to inspect the bus clear to the back rows of seats. Darlene watched him from the oblong mirror above the driver's seat. She could see him bending down and picking up the things she and a boyfriend left behind. She saw his legs approaching, his big hands holding things in front of him as if they were dirty. Thoughts of her quiet uncle upset with her in front of Ben made her skin itch around both her elbows. She scratched each elbow roughly with her chipped nails before Gene confronted her with empty beer cans, Grain Belt, Darlene's father's brand; and Pall Mall cigarette butts placed on top of one can with a used condom on top of another can.

She looked away from the evidence, to outside the cracked window to the gray/green stand of poplars known as Little Woods to locals. She knew that Ben's eyes were on her, too; but it was Gene she could now feel with all her senses as she unconsciously twirled with her thumb and forefinger a peduncle, a stalk from a dandelion she found wedged between her toes.

—Look at me, Gene garbled with a voice strained to be heard above the deluge.

Ben could see that the brown in Darlene's eyes was nearly consumed by a black iris that feared her uncle more than any other person. For she knew he was the only person in the whole world she trusted and who truly loved her the most. Gene's eyes were a blue/green when they were as now, so pinched with a pain between his eyes from his head's motion now in high gear. He said above the rain:

—Is this the kind of life you want, Darlene?

She was far too stubborn to say no or anything when pushed. When he was tired of looking at his niece for some kind of contrition, Gene turned to exit the bus with the evidence to stash it out of sight. That's when Ben started his blush, because the words forming in his throat were moving his tongue, and if he said these words, spit 'em out quick, he could kill the fire that had always consumed him during any possible embarrassing situation.

—Gene? he called out above the rain pelting hard on the tin roof of the bus.

With the salacious garbage held far below his waist in his massive paws, Ben's driver turned back to one of his favorite passengers and walked back to the boy. Looking down at Ben, he listened with his head yet moving fast:

—I would be like Darlene if I was her.

Gene's moving eyes asked why.

—Because that's how she gets to be held..and loved. My mother gives me hugs and kisses all the time.

Darlene began to cry, her quivering chin dipped to her chest, unaware that her beloved uncle was seeing her from a new window made clear by a boy not even ten years old. And Ben felt the fire go out inside him as he watched the back of Gene's small head slow down..more and more until it stayed in a slow motion that Ben had never seen.

Gene reached down and put the dirty things on the aisle floor. Then, he went over to her and gently took the dandelion stem that she was nervously wrapping around her forefinger in order to get her attention.

—Darlene, he whispered.

She looked up at the man who loved her so high above all others as tears streamed down her face.

—Ben's right, he said.

He sat down next to her and held her close, under the pounding liquid marbles that fell on Ledges. When he held her, Ben noticed that Gene's head had stopped moving.

Ben's face turned to the window. He thought he saw a reflection of two strangers where Darlene and Gene are seated. He let it pass as some specter made by the fog and perspiration on his window, unaware of what power emotions have to change a human being. But it was Ben's face that had changed, all from releasing held-in words said to a man he trusted to hear them. Yet, he could not see these changes unless he saw them in a dream..or if he was in some sidereal spin. But it had to be his dream or his spin..or how else could he see it. What is it?

Don't Leave Me

—What is it? Vee mumbled, now conscious that it was her dream..or spin..whatever, as she felt the familiar motion of Traveller on the road.

She could tell she'd slept too long by her sluggish feeling and the kinks in her neck and shoulders. Never could it be proven that she was Darlene Rainbow, so she dismissed the scene in the bu as a dream because she had just read 'Ledges'.

I was listening to a country radio station on low when Vee climbed onto the front passenger seat wearing her light cotton summer pajamas.

—What time is it? she yawned.

—About nine. How'd you sleep?

—I was going to ask you the same thing. I was Darlene again..in a bus with Gene and Ben. Ben made me cry. Were you there?

—No. I got up about four and walked around the farm. When Mr. Olson came out to do chores he let me use his phone. I called Gene's number and a recording told me he's at some county fair in Denison.

—Denison?

—We're almost there.

—Don't you have a signing in Boone tonight?

—I'll make it. Boone's only ninety miles from Denison. How did Ben make you cry?

—He told Gene that I..I mean Darlene sleeps with guys in order to be held and loved. It was strange. Are you sure you weren't there?

—No, I'd tell ya if I was.

—How come I'm alone in these now?

—It was a dream. All yours, baby.

—I've never had a dream as real as that.

—I know. Karen says dreams are more intense when you're in a place you're related to.

—In a past life?

—Yeah. Oh! Don't say anything to Gene about possibly being Darlene in a past life.

—Okay. How long's it been since you've seen him?

—Over thirty-five years.

—So how old would he be now?

—I don't know..60..maybe 65 or 70.

—I'm sure you know that he's the character that made the story in 'Ledges' work so well. Is it true that Gene jumped off that bridge with D.J...and then D.J. jumped at Ledges?

—No. Gene was only our bus driver and Darlene's uncle. His role in 'Ledges' was fiction.

—Then he didn't do Dutch in?

—That's right.

I pointed to the Denison city marker, and got directions to the fairgrounds at a gas station that was an old customer of mine when I was a paper man over twenty years ago.

On the way to the fairgrounds Vee showered and got dressed. She was as anxious as I was to meet my old bus driver. Most importantly to me, I wanted to know if he read 'Ledges' and whether or not he liked it. Of course, I didn't use his real last name, yet I'm sure that anyone who read 'Ledges' in the Boone area would know that Gene was the character Gene in my popular novel.

I wondered if he objected at all to my literary portrait of Gene. And if so, what could I say or do to make amends with a human being I certainly loved during my life on the farm. Or, was Darlene's character (his niece in 'Ledges' and real life) hurtful to Gene.

As I drove north, a couple miles to go before I reached the fairgrounds, I remembered that awful day my sister Karen and I boarded Gene's bus, the day after Darlene and one of her boyfriends were killed in a train accident. They were out parking and drinking at night in the rural cornfields east of Ledges by the main highway when they crossed the railroad tracks and were hit by a freight train. I can vividly remember the first shock upon hearing about it, a jolt far more shocking than any novel could ever be.

Darlene had babysat me and my two sisters several times. She and her uncle made such an impression on me I could not have written 'Ledges' without either of them. Since I wanted to surprise Gene, I left no message on his answering machine. His recording was a woman's voice. I wondered if he could still speak. And if his head still moved from side to side in constant motion. All these things I wanted in Gene's favor; and to finally thank him for inspiring me to write 'Ledges'. Most of all: I selfishly wanted Gene to see me with Vee, because I was like him–alone and introverted so much of my boyhood..when we knew each other.

Plenty of parking was available in an open pasture adjacent the fairgrounds. The overwhelming smells of cooked sausage and bacon coming from a parked motor home next to Traveller increased my hunger for a good country breakfast.

Vee was still getting ready when I stepped outside onto the rich Western Iowa soil. The hills around Denison rolled into neat bands of corn and hay fields. There were splashes of dust in the air from summer gusts of wind that came whipping down from the north over Denison's dry fields in much need of rain.

I didn't tell Vee the truth about how Darlene died in that car/train crash. Never will I forget that it was Gene who told me in a letter that when a young spirit like Darlene's is taken..she will one day return to this world to learn how to live beyond her wild years. I never forgot that letter and the possibilities those words could mean to anyone who experiences loss..until I lost my brother. Gene was the closest I ever came to having a big brother.

From the number of cars parked on the pasture, if Gene was here, he shouldn't be too hard to find. I remembered that his brother and sister-in-law, Darlene's parents had moved here after Darlene was killed. It's still hard for me to believe that people live in the same town for several decades without moving on to experience other places. I wondered why they don't tire of seeing the same faces coming and going.

Just then: Traveller's side door opened, and there was Vee; I hardly recognized her in a dress, a vanilla-cream cotton dress to her ankles. A pair of glittery raspberry slippers were on her small feet. I could see a white bra that covered her small breasts. Her face was so natural with no makeup; her hair was so thick in back and barely touched the nape of her neck. And I just adored how she needed no approval about how she looked. She was saying with her intelligent eyes:

—Here I am. No big deal.

That's exactly how her attitude came across; it was there in her goofy laugh that she never let out unless she liked you when she said:

—I can't remember the last time I wore this.

I took her hand in mine and we walked toward the fairgrounds. Perspiration on her palm told me that she was nervous about meeting Gene. I asked her what she thought about meeting my favorite character in 'Ledges'.

—This Darlene/past life shit has me rattled. In my dream last night..Gene was this loving father figure I or Darlene probably never had. I felt how I..or Darlene disappointed him..hurt him. I've never had that, Dwayne.

—I understand.

Few pedestrians were walking about. It's early yet. The biggest cluster of people were by the 4-H pens and parked trucks with trailers, where farmers, young and old, chatted inaudibly below bawling calves about the upcoming livestock show.

I was looking for a man with a moving head, shaking back and forth, before I realized he might've had an operation, or perhaps he found some medication that made his constant nod cease.

Every eye was on Vee as we walked down a row of makeshift booths for vendors and craftsmen selling everything from art prints to ceramic zebras. I asked a few of them who were still setting up their stands if they happened to know Gene from Boone. Nobody I asked knew him, though I really felt that we would see him any second.

We strolled over to a massive vegetable judging stand where every vegetable under the sun, from beans to watermelons, was scrubbed clean into such glistening color and size that would amaze even the most jaded consumer.

Dozens of fine arts and crafts booths displayed leather work, wood construction, ceramics, creative stitchery, jewelry, hand-crafted dolls, and thousands of wall hangings. I looked closely at each vendor to, hopefully, see that friendly face that safely delivered me and my sister over so many miles to school and back some thirty-five years ago.

Vee was looking, too, but for a different reason. The life she had lived in L.A. as Vicky Derryberry was so much like that of Darlene..it scared her. The only difference: Vee had been given a pretty face. So many times while growing up on the streets of L.A. she felt she was here before in another body, and that the past lessons unlearned in another life are again being thrown at her in this life.

She thought it so ironic that it was in LA. while riding a city bus that the driver told her at age eight about past lives and how that would explain why some innocent children are victims of senseless crimes, poverty and illness, and have terrible circum-stances to deal with. She can still see the face of that bus driver talking to her in his big mirror, saying so casually:

—You don't know what that person did in a past life. That might make sense of it all..and explain the whole rotten mess.

Today, as she stepped slowly with Dwayne, passing a table covered with brilliant crocheted pillow cases and scarves, she realized that the man in 'Ledges' known as Gene Rainbow, could be her only connection to ever having God in her life. Yes, she believed that this character Dwayne had written about could give her a chance to truly love and trust something greater than herself. Until she had faith in some higher power, something to believe in, she would never have a lasting relationship with any man-no matter how much she wanted it.

Vee was certain that it was somehow part of the frightful/

joy that Dwayne talks about, the abject fear of trusting to love again.

　　—I'm gonna go back to Traveller and use my laptop..see if Gene's brother is listed in the phone book. I can't keep askin' everybody out here. You wanna come with me?

　　—No, I'll walk around, Vee said. I might buy something.

　　—Okay. Where should we meet?

　　—I'll come back to Traveller in a half hour or so, she smiled before kissing Dwayne as if she loved him.

For Music and Heat

Vee watched Dwayne until he was out of sight. Fair pedestrians were coming in more and more from the pasture where Dwayne parked Traveller. A radio hanging on a hook above a hot dog stand played golden oldies from the 50s and 60s. She stood near the sound of the music, watching those hard-working, friendly Midwestern people walk by. To her they appeared lost in the ether of their content, as face after face strolled by in groups of two, four and six at a time.

Coming now from the radio was The Marvellettes singing 'Don't Mess With Bill'. It made her think about Billy and Selina, the couple she and Dwayne had spun to in Minneapolis at the Seven Boulders. Just how Billy and Selina were related to them was as big a mystery as Dwayne finding her in Minot and she being the girl from the left-handed town.

That's why she went with Dwayne: to go back to who she was in past lives, and to finally see someone who knew her better than possibly anybody; and it would be someone who was not a past lover, and, if she was Darlene Rainbow: she left him so suddenly, without warning, without telling him goodbye and just how much he meant to her.

Vee looked for Gene while strolling once around the entire fairgrounds, until she returned to Traveller where Dwayne had good news:

—I found him!

—Where?

—His brother was listed and he gave me the number of a friend where I could reach him. He'll be here any minute.

I watched her walk into the bathroom and realized that she was more anxious than I was to see Gene again. And I wanted to call Karen now and tell her how unbelievable it all is, to find that one special person so easily in Minot, who may have been Darlene in a past life, and that Vee was from that left-handed town. But I did not want to be on the phone when Gene arrived.

As I paced Traveller's interior from the kitchen to the recliner my adrenaline was pumping big time, as this will be a past life experience for me–my past life.

My memory gave me shots and scenes of the last time I saw him at the Lake Okoboji Amusement Park. His head was still then, but nobody asked why or how. I had always hoped it would last for him. I wondered if I should tell Gene about Vee possibly being Darlene in not just a past life but in Gene's life. Has he read 'Ledges'? Did he like it?

Just when I thought about going outside to wait for him, there was a light knock at my door. That second: my heart remembered that I once loved this man and it began to beat faster and out of rhythm. I was feeling that same sense of joy..no..that's where it first started, this frightful/joy. It was his. I felt it first with him..and..

—Let me get it, Vee said, heading fast for Traveller's side door. I stepped back, but wanted to position myself to see his first reaction to her.

She opened the door fast. There he was, smiling, with short glistening silver hair and clear blue eyes that did not appear to see any trace of Darlene. Gene's wife Lorraine was standing beside him, smiling with such love in her gray eyes that Vee spoke to them smiling:

—Hi! I'm Vee!

Vee opened the door for them to step up into Traveller.

My eyes widened behind my lenses as they focused on my bus driver from so long ago. The women watched our embrace while Gene laughed as we hugged by the recliner. His head was still. When we separated we gripped each other's arms. Gene spoke slowly:

—Should I call you Ben or Dwayne?

We both laughed hard until I told him that I don't remember ever hearing him laugh before.

—I didn't, Gene laughed.

—I think he's making up for it, Lorraine laughed.

Lorraine sat beside her husband on the sofa as Vee stood next to me after telling me to sit on the recliner. I could tell Vee was staring at Gene as she put her hand on my shoulder as I bathed in this feeling of wonder and awe that Gene was really here.

—I'll bet you were surprised with Dwayne called, Vee said after Gene introduced Lorraine to us.

—Oh yeah, I sure was. How long has it been since I last saw ya?

—Thirty-five..maybe forty years.

Gene shook his head like he used to, but in disbelief and it stopped.

—You look great, Gene, I smiled.

—So do you, Dwayne. How's your mother?

—She's fine. She remarried and lives in Phoenix near Karen.

—How is Karen?

—She has problems with her back and has to be off her feet a lot. She's a librarian.

—Really. She was always a smart girl.

—Yeah, a real smarty, I laughed.

Gene laughed, too. Then Lorraine asked me how my writing was doing, and surprised when she said that she and Gene had read all my books.

—Really? I blinked in wonder. Did you like 'Ledges'? I asked Gene.

Gene began nodding his head and I or Vee didn't laugh until Gene and his wife laughed.

—I really liked it, Dwayne. I'll bet I've told a hundred people to buy it at Hy-Vee or to check it out in the library.

—I'm sold out or I'd give ya a copy.

—Did Karen and your mom like it? Gene asked.

—Yeah. My mom liked it more than Karen. Karen didn't like the parts when she flatulated.

Gene laughed with his wife, then Gene said:

—I'll never forget one time on the bus.. Karen and you always sat behind me..and I heard one of those..loud ones. And I could tell it was Karen because she was laughing so hard but pointing at you. I never saw a boys' face get so red, Gene laughed.

—That's because Darlene thought I did it, I laughed.

Vee could see Gene's eyes brighten from the memory of his niece; and she could see something even Lorraine did not see. She saw it in the bus with Ben when Gene confronted Darlene with the empty beer cans, cigarette butts and used condoms. It was a hurt, a hard one, from when he lost her in that terrible train accident when she was parked in the country.

A wave of rushing compassion came over Vee, until her countenance stunned all of us with such incredible beauty. She had to tell him that she knew Darlene forgave him, and that it was not Gene's fault she parked near those railroad tracks because her uncle confronted her on the bus with that bad stuff. Vee had no clue what to say, but she said this:

—After reading 'Ledges' I have these real dreams about Darlene.

Lorraine and I could see that Vee had Gene's attention, for Vee pointed her words right at him and he could see what she was saying:

—I saw her on an old bus..near Ledges. And you and Ben were there. You were upset about some things you found on the bus.

I could now see Gene's throat bobbing low and rising again under his neck skin, pushing this flush red color from emotion into his face as he listened to this beautiful woman's dream.

—And I can say that I had this feeling that Darlene does not want you to think for one moment that it's your fault for her being in that accident. Something about liking the music from the car radio..and the heater. She thinks you're upset with yourself. It's like she wants you to forgive yourself.

My eyes teared when I saw Gene's hands tremble on his pants atop his knees. Lorraine then put her left hand on her husband's massive right paw.

Just then: Vee sat right on my lap just as Darlene would do whenever she and Gene held each other in order to stop his constant head movement. That's when I could see that Gene's eyes were telling us he was ready to say something he'd never told a soul, even his wife.

—It's true about the bus. When I went to the accident site where Darlene and Roy Jamison were killed..they were just towin' the vehicle away. I looked down...

When Gene's voice faltered..all of us were crying with him as he continued:

—and there on the ground was the same stuff I found on the bus. The same beer cans..her cigarette butts..

We all went over to Gene when he buried his head in his big hands, sobbing like it happened yesterday. Lorraine stroked his neck. I knelt in front of him but Vee pushed me aside and took over the scene like some kind of leading actress in a play.

Lorraine stood after Vee took her hand and helped raise her to her feet. We watched Vee put her hand on the back of Gene's neck that was now a bright red from past emotions flooding his head. When Vee raised Gene's chin with her finger he allowed her to sit on his lap crossways, just as Darlene used to so long ago. I thought I was gonna crap my pants when I saw them there holding each other. To me this reality was more intense than any spin as Lorraine and I watched Gene choke out his words onto Vee's neck:

—I blamed myself for losing you in that accident.

Vee's whisper allowed him to forgive himself:

—It was for music and heat..that's all.

Loraine realized more than I what a relief it was for Gene to be in this state of forgiveness. At that instant, with each convulsing sob of his terribly hard letting go, I could not help but realize how Vee and I, by getting together, had made this moment of healing possible. It was all for my old bus driver, Gene Rainbow. That was when I had the notion that Karen was somehow at the bottom of this healing for Gene. My sister was very fond of Gene when we lived near him, and often talked about him long after we moved away. I dismissed it for the time being.

Lorraine and Gene insisted that Vee and I ride along with them the 18 miles to the Schleswig Steakhouse for lunch.

Lorraine's brother owned the place, and Gene wanted to be around us even more after Vee's help dissolving such an emotional load.

We sat on the back seat of their Buick Skylark, a dark blue sedan that smelled of pine from one of those hanging trees, which I could not see from where I sat. I sat behind Lorraine. Vee wanted to cuddle tight against my side, but we all had to wear our seat belts, so we settled for holding hands between us.

This was the first time I'd seen Vee wear anything other than shorts. She said she had only two dresses and that this one was her only summer dress. Light brown sandals looked so good on her small feet. As we rubbed thumbs I kept thinking about her red heart tattoo while Lorraine talked to Vee about the size of her garden vegetables in Boone. Perhaps it was their combined dialog about organically grown vegetables, and the size of tomatoes, cucumbers and lettuce that somehow mixed with the sweet fragrance Vee was wearing for the first time around me. Anyway, I kept seeing that heart and just knew I could not walk into the restaurant when we parked, especially with my silk shirt tucked into my khaki dress shorts. What made this painful was that Vee knew it was happening and would show me she knew in those eyes that had changed to a more loving color of green; or at least that's what I saw. The best part of it all was that I felt virile and young and lucky as hell to have somehow found a woman who makes me feel this way by no effort whatsoever on her part.

Lorraine asked us how we met. So, I proceeded to tell them about Karen's chart and the spinning back and where it has taken us. Gene and Lorraine could hardly believe what they were hearing. We must've sounded like a couple of gypsies on a peyote or mescaline trip. Yes, we had talked all the way through our prime rib specials before I got around to asking Gene about his life since I moved away.

—I sold my little house in Boone, he said. I had lived there for eleven years.

—Did you still drive a bus and work for the park?

—I drove for three more years before I got hired by the county plowin' snow and servicin' county vehicles. I retired with the county after twenty-five years.

Vee asked them about when they met. Lorraine looked at Gene lovingly before answering:

—I worked in the county Administration Building. Every so often I'd see him.

Gene and Lorraine started to laugh. It was so adorable to watch two people who really love each other and still show it after so many years of marriage. Gene continued:

—One day in February she got caught in a whiteout near Ames and slid into a ditch sideways.

Lorraine laughed so loud with this high pitched squeal as if it was the funniest thing, as Gene continued:

—I came along in a county truck and got her back on the road..

—And it happened again, Lorraine laughed. About a mile down the road it happened again and I ended up back in the ditch.

—Luckily, I saw her, Gene laughed. So I got her out again and made her follow me all the way to work.

—And he asked me out for coffee..if he could drive, she laughed.

—Did he say that..that if he could drive? Vee asked before her goofy laugh.

Lorraine nodded yes while laughing.

On the drive back to Traveller we made plans to have a light dinner at Gene and Lorraine's house in Boone this evening after my signing at the Boone library. Gene and Lorraine wanted to go to the signing so bad that they canceled other plans in Denison.

In Traveller, driving back to Boone, I talked to Vee about when she sat on Gene's lap.

—You really did a good thing for Gene. I hope you know that. Did you see how much better he looked after that?

—Yeah..I truly believe he needed to hear that. It could be the main reason we got together.

—Yeah. The script..Black Hills, Minneapolis..L.A...and now here in this obscure butt crack of the universe..we might have just reached our destiny.

Vee laughed loud and goofy until she said:

—I'd like to go to Okoboji where 'Ledges' ended..and ride that roller coaster.

—We can go there tomorrow.

—Ya know..that script doesn't seem important anymore. I don't feel like finishing it now.

—I know. I feel the same way. You seem happier than usual.

—I started my period today, she smiled.

—Good news, huh?

—No kidding.

The library signing went well in Boone. I sold three dozen books to the forty-some people that showed. Gene tried to buy one, but I gave him one; I signed it: Gene, thanks for your friendship. Your friend always, Dwayne.

At first I felt anxious in the Boone library, since 'Ledges' takes place around Boone and I didn't know how locals felt about it. All went well. The best part was when Vee was seated with Lorraine and Gene near the front and Vee asked me if I was married. My answer drew laughter from the mostly-married audience:

—No..I'm happy.

After a light meal at Gene and Lorraine's house we all sat on lawn furniture in the screened-in porch Gene added on himself. Lorraine asked us where we were headed.

—To Okoboji, Vee smiled. I want to ride the roller coaster.

—I'm not sure it still runs, Gene said.

—I'd like to sell some books up there. And I feel like doing some writing.

—I'll bet it's not very fun for you, Vee, when Dwayne's writing, Lorraine said.

—Oh, I don't mind. I write, too. In fact..I was wanting to write a story with him if he'll let me.

—I'm listening, I said.

Gene said we could park on the street in front of their house for the night, and invited us for breakfast in the morning. It was after we said goodnight to our hosts and sat across from each other at Traveller's booth that we hashed out this collaborative plan: to write a short story about a couple named Mike and Nan. I would write about the first time Mike and Nan meet; Vee would write about the mysterious reason why Nan is in this Midwest town in Cherokee, Iowa. We hammered out the setting and I gave her a verbal tour of the town as I remembered it. We agreed to combine our stories if we thought we had something.

And 'something' had to be romantic with suspense or intrigue in my voice. Third person for Nan's middle. We began writing right away, not knowing what the other was writing. Yes, I would write the beginning; she would write the terrible middle (as in terribly hard); and we would both write the ending.

By the time we had finished, Traveller was parked the next afternoon by Lake Okoboji. Vee had typed it on her word processor. We read silently our story, as we leaned against a giant oak twenty feet from the lake.

To Seduce a Mink

I always saved this stop for last. The Pillow Mink Farm is three miles south of Cherokee in Northwest Iowa. The farm was owned and operated by Gerald Pillow and his family for as long as I could remember.

It's a Thursday, early spring afternoon, and I can recall this place raising minks since the 1950s. My name is Mike Miller. I've been selling paper and janitorial supplies to the Pillow Mink Farm since 1973 when I first started selling for City Paper Company in Sioux City, Iowa.

I'm thirty years old now and lazy compared to when I made my first call here six years ago.

I parked my company van somewhere in the muddy parking area between the upstairs storage area/break room and the dozen or so mud-splattered low mink holding pens that covered ten acres of ground. "Minks stink," I always muttered out loud when I headed on foot to find Gerry the buyer, a top customer for me who always took me upstairs and gave me big orders for product he bought from me every three months.

The break room was empty, and I could see from the remaining supply of my product I would get a nice order from Gerry. But I had to find him first, in one of those long, stinky buildings where the minks lived. My walking shoes were caked with mud so bad that by the time I reached mink house #1 I felt like I was wearing overboots.

No attention was paid to those four-legged stinky rascals by me, thousands of them, that made the Pillows one of the richest families in the area. Of the thirty or so employees that worked here, I saw nobody until I reached the #3 mink house. That's when my life changed forever.

Yes, a girl; yet I couldn't tell what gender until my voice turned her head to me under a red baseball cap she wore backwards. I forgot what I'd asked her when I saw her stunning face. It must've been "Is Gerry around?" because she said:

—Haven't seen him.

She was feeding the penned minks and kits their daily meal of pellets containing some minerals and vitamins that made their fur healthy. Gerry had told me that when I first called on him. Since I felt she was obviously out of my league, maybe eight years younger and far better looking than girls I was used to dating–I had to be funny.

—I'm Mike. I sell Gerry stuff for the break room.
She only nodded in those baggy denim jeans that couldn't hide such a great body I rarely saw in this Heartland zone of corn-fed beef and bacon. I lit a cigarette and offered her one.

—No thanks..I'll have one on my break.

I just stood there watching her overboots move sideways from pen to pen while I crept with her and collected more and more mud on my shoes. I said:

—I should wear boots when I come here.
That's when she looked at my feet and laughed just enough to keep me goin':

—Why do minks stink? I asked her, as she fed one pen with this rubber hose she was pointing and holding with gloved hands.

—It's some chemical from their glands. You'll have to ask Gerry.

—What's your name?

—Nan.

—Short for Nancy?

—No..just Nan.

—You from Cherokee, Nan?

—No.

I probably should've left then, but it was mating season for mink, so something was in the air that made me press.

—I'm spending the night in town..and don't have a clue where to stay..or know any place to go to meet people.

—Can't help ya there. Ask Gerry.

—Okay..see ya, Nan.

—Bye.

I left. By the time I found Gerry pulling up in his pickup by the break room I had told myself a hundred times I'll never meet that beautiful girl again. Gerry was glad to see me. Somehow that didn't help. After I scraped off as much mud as I could, I tramped up the wooden stairs behind Gerry to the storage area/break room.

—I met one of your employees..Nan.

Gerry told me that Nan's from Worthington, Minnesota and that her mother is in the state asylum here after a terrible ordeal he wasn't divulging, or that he wasn't exactly sure about. He was sure that Nan lived alone in town and that she would be here until her mother recovered. When I asked him why he hired someone so transient, he looked right at me and said with that crooked red moustache that drooped and rose with every cynical word:

—You did say you saw her?

It was the first real good laugh I had all day. I was yet writing my two-page order for Gerry when he handed me the greatest favor ever. When he brought me a cup of coffee he said:

—Look, Mike..Nan'll be here for her break in about fifteen minutes. Then, at 4:30 she comes up here to clock out. That's when she calls a cab to take her home. I know she walks to the asylum after she cleans up to have dinner with her mother. A smart young man would offer her a ride.

—She takes a cab every day?

—Five days a week. She's not too friendly with other employees. She keeps to herself. I've given her a ride or two. She's a nice girl..kinda quiet.

—Oh, Gerry..why do minks stink?

—Only the males stink. They're very territorial. They mark their territory.

Gerry left me alone in the break room. I waited at one of the four tables, the one closest to the coffee machine. I had no other calls today. What the hell.

Overboots tramping up the stairs made me pretend to finish writing my twelve hundred dollar order from Gerry, which gave me a total of $1,800.00 in sales for the day. Nan, she just about smiled at me..if not for her mouth not moving. I could tell that her eyes were surprised to see me here.

—Hi, Nan!

She courtesy-waved her hand at me from just below her waist.

I lit a smoke and sat by an open window, taking in the fresh spring air mixed with mink stink. I watched her left hand when it opened the fridge to get a can of Royal Crown Cola. No rings. She sat far enough away from me to let me know that she wasn't very interested in me. I could not let that stop me, not during mink breeding season.

She lit a smoke, too. Good sign.

—Gerry told me that only the males stink.

She nodded while taking a drag, exhaling, and taking a quick sip of RC. I said:

—Why would the guys wanna stink during mating season?

I thanked God she laughed, even adding her words:

—I don't know.

There was something peculiar I noticed right then at that instant; it was in the way she smoked. Worries were what I saw, or rather, her life had been turned upside down by her mother being put away in that imposing asylum known to Iowans as 'Cherokee'. I just had to find out about the whole thing. There's nothing more interesting to me than an attractive woman with a good story. Perhaps it's because I'm a salesman, asking questions all the time to prospects and customers that are ready to tell their story to someone new, someone who will listen.

—Where are you from, Nan? I smiled.

—Worthington.

—Oh, yeah..I've been there. What brings ya to Cherokee?

—My mother's here. I'm visiting her..until she gets better.

—You drive down here?

I knew I was following a line of questioning from clues Gerry had given me, and hoped she didn't catch me or think it caddy.

—My dad brought me.

—How do you get to work?

—A cab.

—That's expensive.

—It's only four bucks each way with a tip.

—That's not too bad. What time you get off?

—Four thirty.

—I'll give ya a ride. I'll be here 'til then anyway.

I thought she was gonna say no, because she looked real smart and had to know that Gerry filled me in.

—Alright.

For a couple minutes she sat there with her thoughts while I traced over my big order from Gerry. When she got up to head back to work I told her I'd see her at 4:30 and that I'd either be up here or outside in my van.

—Okay, she smiled, then hurried downstairs with the grace of a mink.

I got up fast and hustled over to the west window that looked out to the mink barns.

—What a mink, I whispered out loud.

I spent the next half-hour in flashes of images and words, the same way any young man does when he meets a girl he's attracted to, and knows he'll see again..soon. It was glorious time, going over the things I said and she said. The things I said and did that were good or funny, or bad and stupid, was all glorious time. And the way it will be while each part of her beauty is remembered. She will ride in my van and love the music I play. She will be more talkative and laugh more at the things I want her to laugh at. My charm, she will find so irresistible she will invite me inside her apartment where we will kiss for the first time. And she will love me. Yes, these are a single man's thoughts.

At the same time, she will be focused on her work at hand with no other thought in her head about him until she tries to remember his name at the end of her workday. For she will not know if she likes him..until she feels it; that is when she wants him to pursue her—when she knows it. It's always up to her.

Yet something about Nan told me she is not looking or wanting anything to do with the boyfriend routine right now in her life. It was the fact that her mother in that nut house was holding her back from getting close to anyone here.

At 4:30 I was in my van playing The Wallflowers' song 'One Headlight' on my van's CD player. I turned the volume down as she opened my front passenger door, but she turned it back up when she sat down. I kept my mouth shut until the song was over. Then I played the song again. She liked that versus talking to another guy who she thought probably just wanted to boink her. Sure, I wanted to. But that's not all.

Nan was the kind of woman who was out of my league, to me. Again, it's all up to her. Besides, I wasn't one of those drop dead gorgeous guys that can get away with being the silent type and still get the girl. I had to use humor or I was unimpressive..and alone.

During the second time around I had to lower the volume because we hit downtown Cherokee and I like to know when a turn is coming. Not to mention we hadn't said a word to each other since we left the mink farm.

—A left turn at the light, she said.

—You plan on livin' in Cherokee long?

—No, not much longer I hope.

—Why'd you move here?

—You don't have to work me like that.

—What do you mean? I blushed.

—Gerry told me he talked to you earlier about my mother. I don't know if you're a nice guy trying to be nice..or something else. Gerry said you were a nice guy.

—I am.

Before long I knew where we were and asked her if she lived near the sanitarium.

—No.

I waited for more but nothing came.

—Am I dropping you off at the sanitarium?

—Yes, please.

It didn't take a mental giant to see that I'd lost her, and right when the massive dark brick sanitarium came into view on our right. I had to say something:

—Sometimes I eat dinner here..in the cafeteria. The food's not too bad..and inexpensive. I'd love to buy you and your mother dinner here..if she can come.

—She can't.

A long pause as I slowed to 5 mph in the parking lot.

—Can you?

I kept turning my head to her like some anxious caged bird.

—I usually go home and eat when visiting hours are over.

—What time's that?

—Nine.

—How do you get home?

—Cab.

—I'll pick ya up at nine..right here..okay?

She hadn't answered when I double-parked at the entrance doors. Then she said as cold as any delivery:

—I have a boyfriend.

—I'm sure you do. But would he mind or even know if I gave ya a ride home?

—Thanks for the ride, Mike. Bye.

I was pissed all the way to and into my dive motel room at the Cherokee Motor Lodge. Thousands of sales rejections didn't phase me a bit, but this one really bothered me. I just had to see her again. Inside the night stand drawer I pulled out the motel's thin phone book for Cherokee and found one cab company listed.

At 8:30 that night I was parked where I dropped her off in front of that nut house. I was grouchy because I forgot to eat. I was starved.

She could see him saying something to her cab driver before she exited the sanitarium. He had changed into jeans and sandals with a forest green T-shirt.

—That was my cab, Nan said to Mike as the cab left without her.

—I know.

He opened his front passenger door for her with a smile that was not arrogant. She hesitated before getting in, then said:

—I'm hungry.

As he drove to a place he had in mind:

—You didn't eat in the cafeteria?

—No. My mother's not well. Or I should say not improving. She's lost her appetite..and it's hard seeing her get so thin.

—How long has she been here?

—Six months. I've been here for three months.

—Do you mind if I ask what happened to your mother?

—My father died about two years ago..from hospital negligence after bypass surgery. My mother couldn't handle it. They were married for thirty-four years. He was the only man in her life.

—That's too bad.

—Yeah..she's taking it hard because she's the one who talked my dad into having the surgery. It's really awful.

—I'm sorry, Nan. Is she even going to get out of there?

—Not the way it looks. She's so heavily medicated now.. it's a mess.

—You gonna live here much longer?

—I don't want to. But I'm the only child. She's got no friends or relatives. I'm it.

—That's gotta be hard. To give your life up..I mean..I've always resisted my family controlling how or where I live. It's a hard thing to do. I always had trouble with guilt.

—Yeah..that's what I've got goin' on now. I hate guilt.

—Well, I hope things get better for you and your mother.

—Since I moved here I have these dreams that she dies here..and I end up in the same room she had.

—God, Nan, that's scary.

—Yeah.

They ate pizza and shared two pitchers of beer 'til near midnight at a family-owned restaurant in a strip mall north of downtown Cherokee. He told her about his life as a paper salesman and how it was much like her life here where everyone is a stranger with no connections. When Nan asked Mike what he liked to do in his free time, what made him the most happy, his answer caught her off guard, because it was also her passion: writing. He explained:

—When you're a stranger in a town you get the cream of stories you could never imagine. The trick is to write something quick when you see or hear it. I always keep my notebook ready for that.

—Did you write anything today?

—Yeah, in the break room. Wanna read it?

—Yeah.

She watched him more when they drove away from the pizza place and never asked where he was taking her. Reading what he wrote after he first met her would be a good way to find out more about this paper guy, Mike, she thought.

—You work tomorrow? I asked.

—I don't have to be there 'til eleven.

She felt him look over at her; he was looking for a sign that she would be with him tonight.

In his motel room she sat on the bed reading his words. It took her only a minute because it was only one page.

—It reads seductive.

—What do you mean? I asked.

—Well..it's like you're this isolated stud in this small world of yours and you seduce women for your ego. I usually write about things I'm missing or want.

He stood at the end of the bed, numbed with the realization that what she said was true, and it was coming from a stranger that he did want to seduce. She could see his face tighten with anger, the kind of anger that if let out–real self actualization happens. Her father taught her that. Nan let him stew with it until she said:

—You have any toothpicks?

—No.

—There's this bar downtown where we can grab a beer, she said.

Mike said four words from the motel to the bar:

—Where is this place?

Inside the bar, two college guys asked Nan if they'd play pool, partners. Mike nodded yes though he was sulking over Nan's critique of his writing. He wanted to tell her that he wrote what he was feeling at the time and that it had nothing to do with conquest or seduction; in fact, in his words about meeting Nan he felt confident that she would dismiss him and that is why he seduced her on paper.

She knew what she was doing, but he didn't. Flirting with the college boys was turning him off, causing her partner to shoot harder and scratch often. Like most insecure men–Mike's face became uglier during this head game he was losing. Rarely did she flirt, unless she liked someone and played this test on him that he was failing badly. And then came that moment of truth. Would he pass or fail this lesson only girls with balls can teach young men.

She went to the jukebox, selected the most seductive title under the glass Chris Rea's 'On the Beach'. Then came her dance without movement, her backside pointed right at them as she leaned sexily on the jukebox. All a tease. All for show, for only one of the three men who hated it, the one who jumped the cue ball from green felt to cement.

By the time the song was over, she had made him realize exactly what she was doing. Another window. His perspective had changed. She was making him see female seduction and the ensuing insanity it caused insecure men, most men. Seeing her do this, though no attachments to her, was attacking the very core of a big issue, the same issue that turned him away from the world to be a solitary paper man, unable to work for or with others.

So young, yet I wondered how she was so goddam street smart. It had to be that pretty face that had brought a thousand lessons her way.

When she turned away from the jukebox I could see her eyes hunting for me. It was so quick, but my gut feeling was that she really did like me. Our opponents were of no interest to her. After draining three beers in the john I bought the four of us a round, since I scratched on the eight. I told her I wanted to talk to her at a booth.

—If you're going to try to seduce me..I can't help ya there, she laughed.

—I don't think I could if I wanted to. You're too sharp for me.

At a booth off by ourselves she told me that guys who had to be alone with her usually bored her to death with their self-centered talk and other drivel.

—I can understand that. It was really somethin' when I saw you at the jukebox. I could see those two guys, their eyes were all over you. It bothered me. And I really saw what you meant by seduction when you were by the jukebox. It was right there. And it showed me how cold and exploitive seduction is..when you do really like someone.

—What do you mean?

—When two people meet..and when one likes the other first..like me with you..I want you to show me you like me..if you do.

—Oh..and I suppose fucking you would be one way.

—No, no, that never lasts. And that's not what I want.

—What do you want?

—Nothing from you. I want to know if there's anything I can do for you..to help you during this difficult time.

She thought about his words and believed them to be sincere.

—Ya know, Mike..it's kinda like seeing those minks in a cage. I know from being around them that they need space. To see them pacing in circles for hours, day after day, is kinda how I feel being in this town with my life on hold. No matter how many walks I take..beers I drink or daydreams I have about the way I want my life to be...I'm circling in a cage just like those minks do all day and night. But I know in order for me to be free..out of the cage..my mother has to die. And that's what I'm going through. Your little seduction act would be good for me, maybe..if I was really free to experience it. But the way things are..I don't need or want that. It's a nuisance.

—Can you think of anything I can do for you to help you..while you're trapped here?

—No..I appreciate that..but I am here by choice..trapped though it may be. Right now my mother knows I'm here, she knows who I am when I visit her..and she would miss me if I left town.

—You still have to have a life, Nan. I mean..you don't need sex to live..but you have to relate and interact with people and have some friends you can talk to.

—Is that what you do?

—I'm not talking about me. It's different for a man. A man can live without friends or intimacy..maybe not well. But a woman will go insane without connections to people.

—That's exactly what my mother did to herself. My father was her whole world and when he died she died, too. Maybe that's why I resist getting involved.

—Oh..screw involved. I'm talking about just talking..like this. And I'm talking about taking you to Okoboji after work tomorrow after you visit your mother. I'm talkin' about gettin' away..do some lazy fishing, eat in new places and stay in this lakeside motel I know where the trees are so big they can hold both of us against them..as we sit and talk or watch the world go by.

—Now that's seduction, Nan laughed.

—You should laugh more. I like the sound your laugh makes.

—I better get some sleep.

—Yeah, tomorrow's a big day.

—I didn't say I'm going.

—I know. But I am..even if you don't. I can write about seducing you there. Of course, it would be more fun if you were there.

When I dropped her off at her dinky studio apartment, I stayed parked outside until I saw her upstairs light come on. Then I drove away with the sweet smell of her presence still lingering in the late night spring air. I wanted to never return to the life I knew before Nan. I now wanted to stay near this young woman from Worthington, and help her through every day here. And I could imagine us visiting her poor mother as a couple with hope for the future in our eyes.

If she does go with me tomorrow to Okoboji, my past life as a solitary salesman is over, because I will want to be with this girl..I know. I will be with her not only because she is beautiful. And not to seduce her. I will be with her because I must stop this insane circling in my territory, a maddening habit that Pillow minks know. 'Round and 'round from town to town, from one meaningless seduction to another. And in that circle of madness I am swarmed with a thousand limiting beliefs that negate any good desires that could elevate me to better and higher places of consciousness. Innate powers within me will rise when a strong woman like Nan can love me, for if everyone has their own truth, and judgments are tied to beliefs–I will have to leave my circle of madness or she will simply dismiss me.

I slept ten minutes last night, at the most; yet, as I sit in my van near 4:30 at Pillow Mink Farm, I'm more awake than I've been in a long time. As soon as I saw her walking toward me I noticed my finger shivering before I pressed the power button to the van's CD player. But I didn't let that stop me.

'One Headlight' was loud enough for her to know I was back. I so wanted her first reaction to be a smile. It was. As she neared at about 50 yards, while the music made her smile, I decided that even if she didn't go to Okoboji with me, I had to tell her I wanted to see her again. All night long I had laid in bed thinking about the good changes I would make in my life if she went with me today. Putting too much in one basket is dangerous for a paper salesman, because if I'm wrong about her–the circling continues until specious seductions cloud my memory of her and she is gone forever.

About the best thing I inherited from my father was his Irish smile. I used it now when I turned off the music and shouted:

—Hey, Mink Girl!

She held her smile until she walked right up to my van window. Right off the bat my first thought was that she hadn't made up her mind yet about going with me. I listened.

—I can't go..until after my visit with my mom.

—Great! After you clock out I'll give ya a ride home.

As I watched her walk toward the break room my head raced with useless details about motel reservations, getting a nap, my landlady was expecting a rent check from me, and so on.

Then it stopped, the circle of madness. I thought of doing one thing: being someone she can count on for help and understanding, or she will dismiss me to find it in another man. Yes, this Nan from Worthington can teach me how to live in a world far removed from these caged minks at Pillow. I am free. She must see that.

We finished reading our combined short story with our backs against that sturdy oak at that same lakeside motel in Okoboj where Mike wanted to take Nan on their getaway. To sit here beside such a treasure as Vee versus my old days as a paper salesman, and to return to this very spot—was no coincidence.

Our time was more than half over and getting closer to returning to Minot with each thrilling day together going by so fast. Now, I really tried to be with her in the moment with our hands clasped like good friends and lovers. I thought of how good sex was with us, yet we'd only been together a few times. And that was okay, except so foreign to my nature before Minot. My pattern was to wear myself and her out. Consciously I did not know I'd reduced that pattern with this most attractive woman, from my perspective, I've ever been with.

And now, against this sturdy oak, with no signings on my horizon, I told her what I was really feeling. She listened with her eyes on the lake and her left hand in mine just after dusk:

—I feel closer to God after being with you for this short time. And I don't have any fear about saying goodbye to you in Minot. To see Gene again with you has been the best thing in all my travels. I want to take you to my hometown and show you off to every soul that ever knew me there. That would be such a good thing for my ego and self-esteem. Not just because you are beautiful and you have been with me..but because you are a good woman who has helped me remove layers of past emotions that will give me the courage and insight to write again. I thought my next title would be 'Elmwood'. Elmwood is a neighborhood in Woodbury where I spent three years of my youth from ages 10 through 12. Those years had the most impact for creating emotional layers in myself that made me who I am today. I want you to go over every inch of Elmwood with me. And I don't expect you to want to do that with me or go there in-love with me. I want you there..and will pay you a hundred dollars a week, as I told you, for research. In fact, I will give you four hundred when we return to Minot. I have to begin working on my new book in order to generate income when 'Shy Ann is sold out. Again, I want to thank you for a thousand things you've done for me since we met, Vee, and to let you know I hope you are happy about being with me on this journey so that we can both live better in the present.

She said nothing for a long spell. My eyes, too, stayed on the emerald waters as I listened with her hand in mine:

—You are the first man I've ever learned to love without seduction imposed on me. I can tell you've been hurt by chicanery in your past. And I have honestly tried to stay away from that part of me that would surrender myself to you for ulterior motives. I want to go to Elmwood with you because I think I would go anywhere with you..even if you didn't pay me. Yet, I do need money, as you do, and consider that a bonus at this point in my life. That time you heard me with Butch in my room..I was not totally with him. I was in my head about the possibility of what we would be like together. I know that may be a stroke for your ego and sounds like chicanery..but it's a good thing considering who I was before I met you. I try not to think of what will happen when we return to Minot. I don't know how I'll feel then. But right now I'm learning about you and me and enjoying it. When do we go to Elmwood?

—Tomorrow..if you want. After we see about that roller coaster.

We kissed for a long time against that tree, until we ended up in Traveller's bedroom and made love as if we both really loved each other. I'm not one to kiss and tell all the intimate details, but I

-177-

will never think of being with anyone but her..as long as I'm with her.

Though many of my readers and librarians tell me my novel are about interesting characters in interesting situations, I must say I'm feeling lighter these days as I near writing about Elmwood. Since most of the characters in the story are real and alive, I will change their names; and I will consult Karen and her chart to see what it reads for us.

Tomorrow we will drive to Elmwood with Lawn Boy in tow after riding the roller coaster.

Elmwood

I hadn't been home since 'Ledges' was published. As we cruised along Highway 20 onto Gordon Drive, Woodbury hadn't changed much, to me. The beautiful woman riding with me was so incredibly happy to be along that I wanted to stop at every business I recognized, see if some of the same faces worked there, and let them see Vee with me. I knew that this immature desire in me will make sense as I write this story peopled with ghosts in my mind that lived here over forty years ago.

I do not want to bore my readers with my past. I plan to hold their interest by writing about a lost neighborhood, lost youth, and a dysfunctional family in 1962-65 that experienced every possible emotion under God's sun.

—There's the Hy-Vee! I pointed for Vee.

I parked Traveller in the grocery store's large parking lot. Vee went inside the store with me. I took us straight to the book section where I was happy to see that all my books were sold out. One of the friendly cashiers paged Gary the store manager for me while Vee went to the store's deli and ordered us a chicken dinner.

Gary ordered two dozen copies of 'Shy Ann' which I brought in and he paid me cash for. It took me fifteen minutes to sign the books and thank Gary before I joined Vee at a table in the dining area.

—I love quick/easy sales like this, I smiled after filling my cup with Coke at the fountain.

—I love the way you work and live on the road, Vee smiled.

—It's better with you along, believe me, I said while eating my chicken breast.

Vee was smart by picking the best table to people watch, which we both like doing; I guess because we both enjoy writing and seeing things around us. Both of us watched the locals seated around us. I know first hand that these people are some of the hardest working people on earth. Compared to what other Americans get paid for their labor–they can't be happy about it. Meat and feed processing were at one time the largest employers around here. They probably still are, yet the world's largest stockyards is gone, which in one big way is a good thing: The stench in the air from the waste ten thousand new cattle and hogs a day made was always used as a put-down when visitors attacked "Sewer City" they called it.

As a boy I was guilty of the same negative name-calling for my town, and yet, as I grew up I began to call it Superland.

Vee and I could see that most of the colors on their backs were faded colors from hard water and line drying in thick/humid clean air. Jeans are common, though we are in the hottest month-August-when temps are in the 80s and 90s with humidity about as high.

—I'm home, I said while chewing.

—How big is Woodbury?

—Maybe a hundred thousand. It's really a large area in square miles. I think it's one of the biggest counties in Iowa. Iowa, Nebraska and South Dakota converge here. There's gambling in South Dakota, cheaper liquor in Nebraska, and old money in Woodbury.

—You have any people you want to look up?

—No. There's nobody I've stayed in touch with. They have their lives. I'm sure I could spend my time coming and going, but I have too much writing to do.

—I brought my notebook, Vee smiled. I can write things down that we say or see.

—Sounds good.

Vee even wrote things down we didn't see or say. She scribbled notes that were her observations and thoughts about Superland, along with things I mentioned that one of us thought noteworthy. All of that said, I still find it hard to believe I am with someone who is interested in the writing process.

Since the store manager said I could park my RV on his lot

if there was space, and if not, a Wal-Mart was but a few blocks away, parking was handled and off my mind.

I only knew one sure route to get to Elmwood, and that was through the west side all the way down 4th Street, a three-mile roller coaster ride along the sacred Loess Hills where Chief War Eagle is buried.

House after house resembled the one next to it, lower middle class, two-story wood structures painted white mostly with brown window air conditioners dripping water from at least one window per house.

At the bottom of a steep hill the area opened up more so than it did when I lived here, with rows of apartment buildings to our left. On the right, I pointed to where a landmark used to be:

—There used to be an old one-pump gas station there. And there was a traffic light here when I was a patrol boy.

—Patrol boy?

—Yeah..we were like crossing guards for kids.

—What grade were you in?

—Sixth. Only sixth-graders were patrol boys.

Traveller cruised to the highest point on 4th Street, and I was home again, overlooking the valley neighborhood known as Elmwood that was now a half-mile down the winding road and on our left.

—That's Elmwood, I pointed for Vee.

—It looks like a little town.

—In many ways it was.

While cruising downhill, on our left I could see a vast clearing of land that was once dense woods that surrounded War Eagle's Grave. At the bottom of the hill I pointed again for my passenger:

—There used to be an old one-room grocery store there called Conroy's.

Already I was fighting off the memories that were firing in my brain about as fast as Traveller's wheels were turning under us. I turned left just past where the old store used to be and onto the east end of Elmwood, parking soon along the winding-to-the-right

curb just before the first house on the right. After turning off
Traveller's engine Vee asked:

—Did you check what Karen's chart says for this place?

—I didn't want to. I wanted to experience it first and see
then.

—What if there's some real bad stuff on the chart? Wouldn'
you like to know?

—Not really. I got through it the first time.

—That's true.

I let out a very deep sigh and told her what I wanted to do:

—If we take our time it'll take us about two hours to walk
around the neighborhood. Bring your notebook. I'll try to be
spontaneous..and that could mean we visit a house or two..I don't
know. Because of the past..I want you to hold my hand and be as
loving as you can. That way..I know more things will come to me.
If I were alone..I don't think I'd be here now.

—I'll act as if I'm in love with you and interested in every
little thing that happens here.

—I know that would help me write the story.

—Do you have an idea when or how you want the story to
begin?

—Not yet. I thought our walk may bring it out.

—Okay. I'll get some bottled water, she smiled.

After locking Traveller we walked on Elmwood, away from
the sidewalk in order to get a better view. She asked me if this was
where we moved to after we left the farm in Boone.

—Yes.

Our lazy walk down Elmwood into a valley of shade under
century-old elm and oak was more than pleasant. I had somehow
found my way out of the lost path of my youth, a trail that had
short-circuited my life in the present.

Even as we stood in front of my old house and I could truly
imagine my family living there..there was no tension in my body.
Vee suggested we keep walking, up the steep street Oakdale, and
that perhaps I could talk about my life here. But nothing came.

By the time we had circled back to Traveller we had made

plans to explore Minnesota and camp beside some of those ten thousand lakes.

As we cruised up Highway 75 North I felt the afterglow of being in Woodbury and leaving so fast. It reminded me of the thousand towns I left without ever knowing a soul in any one of them. But now, I was not alone. She sat close to me on the passenger seat writing in her notebook that had that candy apple red cover.

—What are you writing?

—About Elmwood, she said without looking up.

When we gassed up in Sheldon and had dinner in a café there, she let me read what she had written:

I wonder now, if I had not been with him would he have begun a great novel from things in his youth re-found. I had learned long ago that what I focus on expands in my life. As we walked all around his boyhood neighborhood Elmwood, I reminded myself nearly every step of the way that he will now experience this place with love and forgiveness in his heart. He did. Nothing came up for him and he decided to scrap the idea of writing a novel about his time spent there. This led me to reason that only love destroys the past; and, that the past is truly dead if love is alive in my life.

Does he love me, too? I think so. I think men are no different in love than women are, no different at all. My past was as bad as his may have been, and yet I don't live in that old negative pattern of cause and effect when I'm with him.

As we head north into Minnesota in this ungodly humidity, I wonder if he will ever write again about his past.

I put down her red notebook and choked down my last swallow of some bitter decaf and said:

—Ever since I met you I've written about what two people experience together. Even if I lose all of my good readers..I want it to stay this way, Vee. Whether we are together or not..I want this connection to the present I seem to have when I'm with you.

Before sunset I parked Traveller beside Round Lake in

Minnesota, not far from an old bait shop/convenience store. An old codger rented me a rod and reel and sold me a dozen worms for the bullheads teeming in the little blue lake.

After sunset Vee awoke from her nap and walked barefoot out to me on this old dock made of dark gray barnwood. I told her I had caught five or six bullheads but tossed 'em all back, using up most of my bait.

—You sure you didn't catch the same fish five or six times? she laughed.

—How are you feeling? I said.

—Tired. A good tired, though, she smiled and sat next to me with her toes testing the cold water.

—When I lived on the farm near Ledges my step-dad brought me here for a couple days one summer.

—Was it a good experience?

—Yes. I remember I cleaned a ton of fish.
I handed her the rod and reel and she liked that, especially when she got quick bites on her line. Then Vee told me about a quick dream she had during her nap:

—You were there. And I was going into one of those spins without you. I ended up fighting it off and staying with you. Then I woke up crying without you there. I was afraid at first..that you were somehow out of my life. I don't know..but I think it's because we're getting closer to Minot.

—What do you think we should do when we get to Minot? I said.

—About us?

—Yeah.

—I don't have any desire to go back to L.A.

—Do you want to stay with me and live this kind of gypsy life?

—Right now I do. I think we need to discuss that.

—From where I sit..I'd like you with me for as long as you want to be with me.

Just then, she got a big bite and excitedly reeled in a nice little bullhead. I pulled out the hook and tossed it back in before I

-184-

kissed her and said:

—I'm hooked, too. Let's agree that whenever one of us wants to change our relationship we talk about it until we are clear about the whole scene.

—Okay, she smiled and kissed me.

After two days of me taking Lawn Boy to nearby towns and selling books door to door to small businesses, we took Traveller north and found other rustic hideaways. It was like a honeymoon everyday for me. We began a new cycle of love making that reached higher levels for both of us. Sometimes three and four times a day.

Our last night before we headed for Minot we stayed in Traveller's bedroom all day going over maps of places we wanted to experience. I felt good about us.

In Minot, I had lunch in Eddie's Café in the hotel and wrote for two hours while Vee met with Butch and their lawyers a half-mile away. When she returned I played our song 'When the Hunter Gets Captured by the Game'; this was right after she told me she got her settlement check and showed me her final divorce papers with her name free and clear of all debts, adding that she was keeping her name as Vee Derryberry.

We kissed sitting next to each other in the booth while the song played. After the song ended she said:

—I'm free to be with you now..all yours, she whispered.

After she said goodbye to a waitress, a cook, and Eddie we walked holding hands back to Traveller under a big blue sky of possibilities. We celebrated by having a candlelit dinner at Traveller's booth with a bottle of good red wine I'd been saving for a time like this.

We made love like minks..free minks..on our way to Arizona to meet my family.

This has been my best summer..this summer of '02. So far, no more spinning back for us. Life is good.

For orders and feedback:

Michael Frederick
P.O. Box 12487
La Jolla, CA 92039
mfrederick310@aol.com